TALES OF UNREST

TALES OF UNREST

BY
JOSEPH CONRAD

"Be it thy course to being giddy minds
With foreign quarrels."
—Shakespeare

GARDEN CITY   NEW YORK
DOUBLEDAY, PAGE & COMPANY
1926

TO
ADOLF P. KRIEGER
FOR THE SAKE OF
OLD DAYS

AUTHOR'S NOTE

OF THE five stories in this volume, "The Lagoon," the last in order, is the earliest in date. It is the first short story I ever wrote and marks, in a manner of speaking, the end of my first phase, the Malayan phase with its special subject and its verbal suggestions. Conceived in the same mood which produced "Almayer's Folly" and "An Outcast of the Islands," it is told in the same breath (with what was left of it, that is, after the end of "An Outcast"), seen with the same vision, rendered in the same method—if such a thing as method did exist then in my conscious relation to this new adventure of writing for print. I doubt it very much. One does one's work first and theorises about it afterwards. It is a very amusing and egotistical occupation of no use whatever to any one and just as likely as not to lead to false conclusions.

Anybody can see that between the last paragraph of "An Outcast" and the first of "The Lagoon" there has been no change of pen, figuratively speaking. It happens also to be literally true. It was the same pen: a common steel pen. Having been charged with a certain lack of emotional faculty I am glad to be able to say that on one occasion at least I did give way to a sentimental impulse. I thought the pen had been a good pen and that it had done enough for me, and so, with the idea of keeping it for a sort of memento on which I could look later with tender eyes, I put it into my waistcoat pocket. Afterwards it used to turn up in all sorts of places—at the bottom of small drawers, among my studs in cardboard boxes—till at last it found permanent rest in a large wooden bowl containing some loose keys, bits of sealing wax, bits of string, small broken chains, a few buttons, and similar minute wreckage that washes out of a man's life into such receptacles. I would catch sight of it from time to time with a distinct feeling of satisfaction till, one day, I perceived with horror that there were two old pens in there. How the other pen found its way into the bowl instead of the fireplace or wastepaper basket I can't imagine, but there the two were, lying side by side, both encrusted with ink and completely undistinguishable from each other. It was very distressing, but being determined not to share my sentiment between two pens or run the risk of sentimentalising over a mere stranger, I threw them both out of the window into a flower bed—which strikes me now as a poetical grave for the remnants of one's past.

But the tale remained. It was first fixed in print in the *Cornhill Magazine*, being my first appearance in a serial of any kind; and I have lived long enough to see it guyed most agreeably by Mr. Max Beerbohm in a volume of parodies entitled *A Christmas Garland*, where I found myself in very good company. I was immensely gratified. I began to believe in my public existence. I have much to thank "The Lagoon" for.

My next effort in short-story writing was a departure —I mean a departure from the Malay Archipelago. Without premeditation, without sorrow, without rejoicing, and almost without noticing it, I stepped into the very different atmosphere of "An Outpost of Progress." I found there a different moral attitude. I seemed able to capture new reactions, new suggestions, and even new rhythms for my paragraphs. For a

moment I fancied myself a new man—a most exciting
illusion. It clung to me for some time, monstrous, half
conviction and half hope as to its body, with an irides-
cent tail of dreams and with a changeable head like a
plastic mask. It was only later that I perceived that
in common with the rest of men nothing could deliver
me from my fatal consistency. We cannot escape from
ourselves.

"An Outpost of Progress" is the lightest part of the
loot I carried off from Central Africa, the main portion
being of course "The Heart of Darkness." Other men
have found a lot of quite different things there and I
have the comfortable conviction that what I took would
not have been of much use to anybody else. And it
must be said that it was but a very small amount of
plunder. All of it could go into one's breast pocket
when folded neatly. As for the story itself it is true
enough in its essentials. The sustained invention of a
really telling lie demands a talent which I do not possess.

"The Idiots" is such an obviously derivative piece of
work that it is impossible for me to say anything about
it here. The suggestion of it was not mental but visual:
the actual idiots. It was after an interval of long groping amongst vague impulses and hesitations which
ended in the production of "The Nigger" that I turned
to my third short story in the order of time, the first
in this volume: "Karain: A Memory."

Reading it after many years "Karain" produced on
me the effect of something seen through a pair of glasses
from a rather advantageous position. In that story I
had not gone back to the Archipelago, I had only turned
for another look at it. I admit that I was absorbed
by the distant view, so absorbed that I didn't notice
then that the *motif* of the story is almost identical with
the *motif* of "The Lagoon." However, the idea at the

back is very different; but the story is mainly made memorable to me by the fact that it was my first contribution to *Blackwood's Magazine* and that it led to my personal acquaintance with Mr. William Blackwood whose guarded appreciation I felt nevertheless to be genuine, and prized accordingly. "Karain" was begun on a sudden impulse only three days after I wrote the last line of "The Nigger," and the recollection of its difficulties is mixed up with the worries of the unfinished "Return," the last pages of which I took up again at the time; the only instance in my life when I made an attempt to write with both hands at once as it were.

Indeed my innermost feeling, now, is that "The Return" is a left-handed production. Looking through that story lately I had the material impression of sitting under a large and expensive umbrella in the loud drumming of a heavy rain-shower. It was very distracting. In the general uproar one could hear every individual drop strike on the stout and distended silk. Mentally, the reading rendered me dumb for the remainder of the day, not exactly with astonishment but with a sort of dismal wonder. I don't want to talk disrespectfully of any pages of mine. Psychologically there were no doubt good reasons for my attempt; and it was worth while, if only to see of what excesses I was capable in that sort of virtuosity. In this connection I should like to confess my surprise on finding that notwithstanding all its apparatus of analysis the story consists for the most part of physical impressions; impressions of sound and sight, railway station, streets, a trotting horse, reflections in mirrors and so on, rendered as if for their own sake and combined with a sublimated description of a desirable middle-class town-residence which somehow manages to produce a sinister effect. For the rest any kind word about "The Return" (and there have

been such words said at different times) awakens in the
the liveliest gratitude, for I know how much the writing
of that fantasy has cost me in sheer toil, in temper, and
in disillusion.

J. C.

CONTENTS

TALES OF UNREST

TALES OF UNREST

KARAIN: A MEMORY

I

WE KNEW him in those unprotected days when we were content to hold in our hands our lives and our property. None of us, I believe, has any property now, and I hear that many, negligently, have lost their lives; but I am sure that the few who survive are not yet so dim-eyed as to miss in the befogged respectability of their newspapers the intelligence of various native risings in the Eastern Archipelago. Sunshine gleams between the lines of those short paragraphs—sunshine and the glitter of the sea. A strange name wakes up memories; the printed words scent the smoky atmosphere of to-day faintly, with the subtle and penetrating perfume as of land breezes breathing through the starlight of bygone nights; a signal fire gleams like a jewel on the high brow of a sombre cliff; great trees, the advanced sentries of immense forests, stand watchful and still over sleeping stretches of open water; a line of white surf thunders on an empty beach, the shallow water foams on the reefs; and green islets scattered through the calm of noonday lie upon the level of a polished sea, like a handful of emeralds on a buckler of steel.

There are faces too—faces dark, truculent, and smiling; the frank audacious faces of men barefooted, well

armed and noiseless. They thronged the narrow length
of our schooner's decks with their ornamented and barbarous crowd, with the variegated colours of checkered
sarongs, red turbans, white jackets, embroideries; with
the gleam of scabbards, gold rings, charms, armlets,
lance blades, and jewelled handles of their weapons.
They had an independent bearing, resolute eyes, a restrained manner; and we seem yet to hear their soft
voices speaking of battles, travels, and escapes; boast-
ing with composure, joking quietly; sometimes in well-
bred murmurs extolling their own valour, our generosity; or celebrating with loyal enthusiasm the virtues
of their ruler. We remember the faces, the eyes, the
voices, we see again the gleam of silk and metal; the
murmuring stir of that crowd, brilliant, festive, and
martial; and we seem to feel the touch of friendly
brown hands that, after one short grasp, return to rest
on a chased hilt. They were Karain's people—a
devoted following. Their movements hung on his
lips; they read their thoughts in his eyes; he murmured
to them nonchalantly of life and death, and they accepted his words humbly, like gifts of fate. They were
all free men, and when speaking to him said, "Your
slave." On his passage voices died out as though he
had walked guarded by silence; awed whispers followed
him. They called him their war-chief. He was the
ruler of three villages on a narrow plain; the master
of an insignificant foothold on the earth—of a conquered
foothold that, shaped like a young moon, lay ignored
between the hills and the sea.

From the deck of our schooner, anchored in the
middle of the bay, he indicated by a theatrical sweep
of his arm along the jagged outline of the hills the
whole of his domain; and the ample movement seemed
to drive back its limits, augmenting it suddenly into

something so immense and vague that for a moment it appeared to be bounded only by the sky. And really, looking at that place, landlocked from the sea and shut off from the land by the precipitous slopes of mountains, it was difficult to believe in the existence of any neighbourhood. It was still, complete, unknown, and full of a life that went on stealthily with a troubling effect of solitude; of a life that seemed unaccountably empty of anything that would stir the thought, touch the heart, give a hint of the ominous sequence of days. It appeared to us a land without memories, regrets, and hopes; a land where nothing could survive the coming of the night, and where each sunrise, like a dazzling act of special creation, was disconnected from the eve and the morrow.

Karain swept his hand over it. "All mine!" He struck the deck with his long staff; the gold head flashed like a falling star; very close behind him a silent old fellow in a richly embroidered black jacket alone of all the Malays around did not follow the masterful gesture with a look. He did not even lift his eyelids. He bowed his head behind his master, and without stirring held hilt up over his right shoulder a long blade in a silver scabbard. He was there on duty, but without curiosity, and seemed weary, not with age, but with the possession of a burdensome secret of existence. Karain, heavy and proud, had a lofty pose and breathed calmly. It was our first visit, and we looked about curiously.

The bay was like a bottomless pit of intense light. The circular sheet of water reflected a luminous sky, and the shores enclosing it made an opaque ring of earth floating in an emptiness of transparent blue. The hills, purple and arid, stood out heavily on the sky: their summits seemed to fade into a coloured tremble

as of ascending vapour; their steep sides were streaked
with the green of narrow ravines; at their foot lay rice-
fields, plantain-patches, yellow sands. A torrent wound
about like a dropped thread. Clumps of fruit-trees
marked the villages; slim palms put their nodding heads
together above the low houses; dried palm-leaf roofs
shone afar, like roofs of gold, behind the dark colon-
nades of tree-trunks; figures passed vivid and vanish-
ing; the smoke of fires stood upright above the masses
of flowering bushes; bamboo fences glittered, running
away in broken lines between the fields. A sudden
cry on the shore sounded plaintive in the distance,
and ceased abruptly, as if stifled in the downpour of
sunshine. A puff of breeze made a flash of darkness
on the smooth water, touched our faces, and became
forgotten. Nothing moved. The sun blazed down
into a shadowless hollow of colours and stillness.

It was the stage where, dressed splendidly for his
part, he strutted, incomparably dignified, made important by the power he had to awaken an absurd
expectation of something heroic going to take place—
a burst of action or song—upon the vibrating tone of a
wonderful sunshine. He was ornate and disturbing,
for one could not imagine what depth of horrible void
such an elaborate front could be worthy to hide. He
was not masked—there was too much life in him, and
a mask is only a lifeless thing; but he presented himself essentially as an actor, as a human being aggres-
sively disguised. His smallest acts were prepared and
unexpected, his speeches grave, his sentences ominous
like hints and complicated like arabesques. He was
treated with a solemn respect accorded in the irreverent
West only to the monarchs of the stage, and he accepted
the profound homage with a sustained dignity seen
nowhere else but behind the footlights and in the con-

densed falseness of some grossly tragic situation. It was almost impossible to remember who he was— only a petty chief of a conveniently isolated corner of Mindanao, where we could in comparative safety break the law against the traffic in firearms and ammunition with the natives. What would happen should one of the moribund Spanish gun-boats be suddenly galvanized into a flicker of active life did not trouble us, once we were inside the bay—so completely did it appear out of the reach of a meddling world; and besides, in those days we were imaginative enough to look with a kind of joyous equanimity on any chance there was of being quietly hanged somewhere out of the way of diplomatic remonstrance. As to Karain, nothing could happen to him unless what happens to all—failure and death; but his quality was to appear clothed in the illusion of unavoidable success. He seemed too effective, too necessary there, too much of an essential condition for the existence of his land and his people, to be destroyed by anything short of an earthquake. He summed up his race, his country, the elemental force of ardent life, of tropical nature. He had its luxuriant strength, its fascination; and, like it, he carried the seed of peril within.

In many successive visits we came to know his stage well—the purple semicircle of hills, the slim trees leaning over houses, the yellow sands, the streaming green of ravines. All that had the crude and blended colouring, the appropriateness almost excessive, the suspicious immobility of a painted scene; and it enclosed so perfectly the accomplished acting of his amazing pretences that the rest of the world seemed shut out forever from the gorgeous spectacle. There could be nothing outside. It was as if the earth had gone on spinning, and had left that crumb of its surface alone in space. He appeared utterly cut off from everything but the sunshine, and that even seemed to be made for him alone. Once when asked what was on the other side of the hills, he said, with a meaning smile, "Friends and enemies—many enemies; else why should I buy your rifles and powder?" He was always like this— word-perfect in his part, playing up faithfully to the mysteries and certitudes of his surroundings. "Friends and enemies"—nothing else. It was impalpable and vast. The earth had indeed rolled away from under his land, and he, with his handful of people, stood surrounded by a silent tumult as of contending shades. Certainly no sound came from outside. "Friends and enemies!" He might have added, "and memories," at least as far as he himself was concerned; but he neglected to make that point then. It made itself later on, though; but it was after the daily performance—in the wings, so to speak, and with the lights out. Meantime he filled the stage with barbarous dignity. Some ten years ago he had led his people —a scratch lot of wandering Bugis—to the conquest of the bay, and now in his august care they had forgotten all the past, and had lost all concern for the future. He gave them wisdom, advice, reward, punishment, life or death, with the same serenity of attitude and voice. He understood irrigation and the art of war—the qualities of weapons and the craft of boatbuilding. He could conceal his heart; had more endurance; he could swim longer, and steer a canoe better than any of his people; he could shoot straighter, and negotiate more tortuously than any man of his race I knew. He was an adventurer of the sea, an outcast, a ruler—and my very good friend. I wish him a quick death in a stand-up fight, a death in sunshine; for he had known remorse and power, and no man can demand more from life. Day after day he appeared before us, incomparably faithful to the illusions of the stage, and at sunset the night descended upon him quickly, like a falling curtain. The seamed hills became black shadows towering high upon a clear sky; above them the glittering confusion of stars resembled a mad turmoil stilled by a gesture; sounds ceased, men slept, forms vanished—and the reality of the universe alone remained—a marvellous thing of darkness and glimmers.

II

But it was at night that he talked openly, forgetting the exactions of his stage. In the daytime there were affairs to be discussed in state. There were at first between him and me his own splendour, my shabby suspicions, and the scenic landscape that intruded upon the reality of our lives by its motionless fantasy of outline and colour. His followers thronged round him; above his head the broad blades of their spears made a spiked halo of iron points, and they hedged him from humanity by the shimmer of silks, the gleam of weapons, the excited and respectful hum of eager voices. Before sunset he would take leave with ceremony, and go off sitting under a red umbrella, and escorted by a score of boats. All the paddles flashed and struck together with a mighty splash that reverberated loudly in the monumental amphitheatre of hills. A broad stream of dazzling foam trailed behind the flotilla. The canoes appeared very black on the white hiss of water; turbaned heads swayed back and forth; a multitude of arms in crimson and yellow rose and fell with one movement; the spearmen upright in the bows of canoes had variegated sarongs and gleaming shoulders like bronze statues; the muttered strophes of the paddlers' song ended periodically in a plaintive shout. They diminished in the distance; the song ceased; they swarmed on the beach in the long shadows of the western hills. The sunlight lingered on the purple crests, and we could see him leading the way to his stockade, a burly bareheaded figure walking far in advance of a straggling *cortège*, and swinging regularly an ebony staff taller than himself. The darkness deepened fast; torches gleamed fitfully, passing behind bushes; a long hail or two trailed in the silence of the evening; and at last the night stretched its smooth veil over the shore, the lights, and the voices.

Then, just as we were thinking of repose, the watch-men of the schooner would hail a splash of paddles away in the starlit gloom of the bay; a voice would respond in cautious tones, and our serang, putting his head down the open skylight, would inform us without surprise, "That Rajah, he coming. He here now." Karain appeared noiselessly in the doorway of the little cabin. He was simplicity itself then; all in white; muffled about his head; for arms only a kriss with a plain buffalo-horn handle, which he would politely conceal within a fold of his sarong before stepping over the threshold. The old sword-bearer's face, the worn-out and mournful face so covered with wrinkles that it seemed to look out through the meshes of a fine dark net, could be seen close above his shoulders. Karain never moved without that attendant, who stood or squatted close at his back. He had a dislike of an open space behind him. It was more than a dislike —it resembled fear, a nervous preoccupation of what went on where he could not see. This, in view of the evident and fierce loyalty that surrounded him, was inexplicable. He was there alone in the midst of devoted men; he was safe from neighbourly am-bushes, from fraternal ambitions; and yet more than one of our visitors had assured us that their ruler could not bear to be alone. They said, "Even when he eats and sleeps there is always one on the watch near him who has strength and weapons." There was indeed always one near him, though our informants had no conception of that watcher's strength and weapons, which were both shadowy and terrible. We knew, but only later on, when we had heard the story. Meantime we noticed that, even during the most important interviews, Karain would often give a start, and interrupting his discourse, would sweep his arm back with a sudden movement, to feel whether the old fellow was there. The old fellow, impenetrable and weary, was always there. He shared his food, his repose, and his thoughts; he knew his plans, guarded his secrets; and, impassive behind his master's agitation, without stirring the least bit, murmured above his head in a soothing tone some words difficult to catch.

It was only on board the schooner, when surrounded by white faces, by unfamiliar sights and sounds, that Karain seemed to forget the strange obsession that wound like a black thread through the gorgeous pomp of his public life. At night we treated him in a free and easy manner, which just stopped short of slapping him on the back, for there are liberties one must not take with a Malay. He said himself that on such occasions he was only a private gentleman coming to see other gentlemen whom he supposed as well born as himself. I fancy that to the last he believed us to be emissaries of Government, darkly official persons furthering by our illegal traffic some dark scheme of high statecraft. Our denials and protestations were unavailing. He only smiled with discreet politeness and inquired about the Queen. Every visit began with that inquiry; he was insatiable of details; he was fascinated by the holder of a sceptre the shadow of which, stretching from the westward over the earth and over the seas, passed far beyond his own hand's-breadth of conquered land. He multiplied questions; he could never know enough of the Monarch of whom he spoke with wonder and chivalrous respect—with a kind of affectionate awe! Afterwards, when we had learned that he was the son of a woman who had many years ago ruled a small Bugis state, we came to suspect that the memory of his mother (of whom he spoke with enthusiasm) mingled somehow in his mind with the image he tried to form for himself of the far-off Queen whom he called Great, Invincible, Pious, and Fortunate. We had to invent details at last to satisfy his craving curiosity; and our loyalty must be pardoned, for we tried to make them fit for his august and resplendent ideal. We talked. The night slipped over us, over the still schooner, over the sleeping land, and over the sleepless sea that thundered amongst the reefs outside the bay. His paddlers, two trustworthy men, slept in the canoe at the foot of our side-ladder. The old confidant, relieved from duty, dozed on his heels, with his back against the companion-doorway; and Karain sat squarely in the ship's wooden armchair, under the slight sway of the cabin lamp, a cheroot between his dark fingers, and a glass of lemonade before him. He was amused by the fizz of the thing, but after a sip or two would let it get flat, and with a courteous wave of his hand ask for a fresh bottle. He decimated our slender stock; but we did not begrudge it to him, for, when he began, he talked well. He must have been a great Bugis dandy in his time, for even then (and when we knew him he was no longer young) his splendour was spotlessly neat, and he dyed his hair a light shade of brown. The quiet dignity of his bearing transformed the dim-lit cuddy of the schooner into an audience-hall. He talked of inter-island politics with an ironic and melancholy shrewdness. He had travelled much, suffered not a little, intrigued, fought. He knew native Courts, European Settlements, the forests, the sea, and, as he said himself, had spoken in his time to many great men. He liked to talk with me because I had known some of these men: he seemed to think that I could understand him, and, with a fine confidence, assumed that I, at least, could appreciate how much greater he was himself. But he preferred to talk of his native country—a small Bugis state on the island of Celebes. I had visited it some time before, and he asked eagerly for news. As men's names came up in conversation he would say, "We swam against one another when we were boys"; or, "We hunted the deer together—he could use the noose and the spear as well as I." Now and then his big dreamy eyes would roll restlessly; he frowned or smiled, or he would become pensive, and, staring in silence, would nod slightly for a time at some regretted vision of the past.

His mother had been the ruler of a small semi-independent state on the sea-coast at the head of the Gulf of Boni. He spoke of her with pride. She had been a woman resolute in affairs of state and of her own heart. After the death of her first husband, undismayed by the turbulent opposition of the chiefs, she married a rich trader, a Korinchi man of no family. Karain was her son by that second marriage, but his unfortunate descent had apparently nothing to do with his exile. He said nothing as to its cause, though once he let slip with a sigh, "Ha! my land will not feel any more the weight of my body." But he related willingly the story of his wanderings, and told us all about the conquest of the bay. Alluding to the people beyond the hills, he would murmur gently, with a careless wave of the hand, "They came over the

hills once to fight us, but those who got away never
came again." He thought for a while, smiling to
himself. "Very few got away," he added, with proud
serenity. He cherished the recollections of his successes; he had an exulting eagerness for endeavour;
when he talked, his aspect was warlike, chivalrous,
and uplifting. No wonder his people admired him.
We saw him once walking in daylight amongst the
houses of the settlement. At the doors of huts groups
of women turned to look after him, warbling softly,
and with gleaming eyes; armed men stood out of the
way, submissive and erect; others approached from
the side, bending their backs to address him humbly;
an old woman stretched out a draped lean arm—
"Blessings on thy head!" she cried from a dark doorway;
a fiery-eyed man showed above the low fence of a
plantain-patch a streaming face, a bare breast scarred
in two places, and bellowed out pantingly after him,
"God give victory to our master!" Karain walked
fast, and with firm long strides; he answered greetings
right and left by quick piercing glances. Children
ran forward between the houses, peeped fearfully
round corners; young boys kept up with him, gliding
between bushes: their eyes gleamed through the dark
leaves. The old sword-bearer, shouldering the silver
scabbard, shuffled hastily at his heels with bowed
head, and his eyes on the ground. And in the midst of a
great stir they passed swift and absorbed, like two men
hurrying through a great solitude.

In his council hall he was surrounded by the gravity
of armed chiefs, while two long rows of old headmen
dressed in cotton stuffs squatted on their heels, with
idle arms hanging over their knees. Under the thatch
roof supported by smooth columns, of which each one
had cost the life of a straight-stemmed young palm,

the scent of flowering hedges drifted in warm waves. The sun was sinking. In the open courtyard suppliants walked through the gate, raising, when yet far off, their joined hands above bowed heads, and bending low in the bright stream of sunlight. Young girls, with flowers in their laps, sat under the wide-spreading boughs of a big tree. The blue smoke of wood fires spread in a thin mist above the high-pitched roofs of houses that had glistening walls of woven reeds, and all round them rough wooden pillars under the sloping eaves. He dispensed justice in the shade; from a high seat he gave orders, advice, reproof. Now and then the hum of approbation rose louder, and idle spearmen that lounged listlessly against the posts, looking at the girls, would turn their heads slowly. To no man had been given the shelter of so much respect, confidence, and awe. Yet at times he would lean forward and appear to listen as for a far-off note of discord, as if expecting to hear some faint voice, the sound of light footsteps; or he would start half up in his seat, as though he had been familiarly touched on the shoulder. He glanced back with apprehension; his aged follower whispered inaudibly at his ear; the chiefs turned their eyes away in silence, for the old wizard, the man who could command ghosts and send evil spirits against enemies, was speaking low to their ruler. Around the short stillness of the open place the trees rustled faintly, the soft laughter of girls playing with the flowers rose in clear bursts of joyous sound. At the end of upright spear-shafts the long tufts of dyed horse-hair waved crimson and filmy in the gust of wind and beyond the blaze of hedges the brook of limpid quick water ran invisible and loud under the drooping grass of the bank, with a great murmur, passionate and gentle.

After sunset, far across the fields and over the bay, clusters of torches could be seen burning under the high roofs of the council shed. Smoky red flames swayed on high poles, and the fiery blaze flickered over faces, clung to the smooth trunks of palm-trees, kindled bright sparks on the rims of metal dishes standing on fine floor-mats. That obscure adventurer feasted like a king. Small groups of men crouched in tight circles round the wooden platters; brown hands hovered over snowy heaps of rice. Sitting upon a rough couch apart from the others, he leaned on his elbow with inclined head; and near him a youth improvised in a high tone a song that celebrated his valour and wisdom. The singer rocked himself to and fro, rolling frenzied eyes; old women hobbled about with dishes, and men, squatting low, lifted their heads to listen gravely without ceasing to eat. The song of triumph vibrated in the night, and the stanzas rolled out mournful and fiery like the thoughts of a hermit. He silenced it with a sign, "Enough!" An owl hooted far away, exulting in the delight of deep gloom in dense foliage; overhead lizards ran in the attap thatch, calling softly; the dry leaves of the roof rustled; the rumour of mingled voices grew louder suddenly. After a circular and startled glance, as of a man waking up abruptly to the sense of danger, he would throw himself back, and under the downward gaze of the old sorcerer take up, wide-eyed, the slender thread of his dream. They watched his moods; the swelling rumour of animated talk subsided like a wave on a sloping beach. The chief is pensive. And above the spreading whisper of lowered voices only a light rattle of weapons would be heard, a single louder word distinct and alone, or the grave ring of a big brass tray.

III

For two years at short intervals we visited him.
We came to like him, to trust him, almost to admire
him. He was plotting and preparing a war with patience, with foresight—with a fidelity to his purpose
and with a steadfastness of which I would have thought
him racially incapable. He seemed fearless of the
future, and in his plans displayed a sagacity that was
only limited by his profound ignorance of the rest of
the world. We tried to enlighten him, but our attempts
to make clear the irresistible nature of the forces which
he desired to arrest failed to discourage his eagerness
to strike a blow for his own primitive ideas. He did
not understand us, and replied by arguments that
almost drove one to desperation by their childish
shrewdness. He was absurd and unanswerable. Sometimes we caught glimpses of a sombre, glowing fury within him—a brooding and vague sense of wrong, and a
concentrated lust of violence which is dangerous in a
native. He raved like one inspired. On one occasion,
after we had been talking to him late in his campong,
he jumped up. A great, clear fire blazed in the grove;
lights and shadows danced together between the trees;
in the still night bats flitted in and out of the boughs
like fluttering flakes of denser darkness. He snatched
the sword from the old man, whizzed it out of the
scabbard, and thrust the point into the earth. Upon
the thin, upright blade the silver hilt, released, swayed
before him like something alive. He stepped back a

18

pace, and in a deadened tone spoke fiercely to the vibrating steel: "If there is virtue in the fire, in the iron, in the hand that forged thee, in the words spoken over thee, in the desire of my heart, and in the wisdom of thy makers,—then we shall be victorious together!" He drew it out, looked along the edge. "Take," he said over his shoulder to the old sword-bearer. The other, unmoved on his hams, wiped the point with a corner of his sarong, and returning the weapon to its scabbard, sat nursing it on his knees without a single look upwards. Karain, suddenly very calm, re-seated himself with dignity. We gave up remonstrating after this, and let him go his way to an honourable disaster. All we could do for him was to see to it that the powder was good for the money and the rifles serviceable, if old.

But the game was becoming at last too dangerous; and if we, who had faced it pretty often, thought little of the danger, it was decided for us by some very respectable people sitting safely in counting-houses that the risks were too great, and that only one more trip could be made. After giving in the usual way many misleading hints as to our destination, we slipped away quietly, and after a very quick passage entered the bay. It was early morning, and even before the anchor went to the bottom the schooner was surrounded by boats.

The first thing we heard was that Karain's mysterious sword-bearer had died a few days ago. We did not attach much importance to the news. It was certainly difficult to imagine Karain without his inseparable follower; but the fellow was old, he had never spoken to one of us, we hardly ever had heard the sound of his voice; and we had come to look upon him as upon something inanimate, as a part of our friend's trappings of state—like that sword he had carried, or the fringed red umbrella displayed during an official progress. Karain did not visit us in the afternoon as usual. A message of greeting and a present of fruit and vegetables came off for us before sunset. Our friend paid us like a banker, but treated us like a prince. We sat up for him till midnight. Under the stern awning bearded Jackson jingled an old guitar and sang, with an execrable accent, Spanish love-songs; while young Hollis and I, sprawling on the deck, had a game of chess by the light of a cargo lantern. Karain did not appear. Next day we were busy unloading, and heard that the Rajah was unwell. The expected invitation to visit him ashore did not come. We sent friendly messages, but, fearing to intrude upon some secret council, remained on board. Early on the third day we had landed all the powder and rifles, and also a six-pounder brass gun with its carriage which we had subscribed together for a present for our friend. The afternoon was sultry. Ragged edges of black clouds peeped over the hills, and invisible thunderstorms circled outside, growling like wild beasts. We got the schooner ready for sea, intending to leave next morning at daylight. All day a merciless sun blazed down into the bay, fierce and pale, as if at white heat. Nothing moved on the land. The beach was empty, the villages seemed deserted; the trees far off stood in unstirring clumps, as if painted; the white smoke of some invisible bush-fire spread itself low over the shores of the bay like a settling fog. Late in the day three of Karain's chief men, dressed in their best and armed to the teeth, came off in a canoe, bringing a case of dollars. They were gloomy and languid, and told us they had not seen their Rajah for five days. No one had seen him! We settled all accounts, and after shaking hands in turn and in profound silence, they descended one after another into their boat, and were paddled to the shore, sitting close together, clad in vivid colours, with hanging heads: the gold embroideries of their jackets flashed dazzlingly as they went away gliding on the smooth water, and not one of them looked back once. Before sunset the growling clouds carried with a rush the ridge of hills, and came tumbling down the inner slopes. Everything disappeared; black whirling vapours filled the bay, and in the midst of them the schooner swung here and there in the shifting gusts of wind. A single clap of thunder detonated in the hollow with a violence that seemed capable of bursting into small pieces the ring of high land, and a warm deluge descended. The wind died out. We panted in the close cabin; our faces streamed; the bay outside hissed as if boiling; the water fell in perpendicular shafts as heavy as lead; it swished about the deck, poured off the spars, gurgled, sobbed, splashed, murmured in the blind night. Our lamp burned low. Hollis, stripped to the waist, lay stretched out on the lockers, with closed eyes and motionless like a despoiled corpse; at his head Jackson twanged the guitar, and gasped out in sighs a mournful dirge about hopeless love and eyes like stars. Then we heard startled voices on deck crying in the rain, hurried footsteps overhead, and suddenly Karain appeared in the doorway of the cabin. His bare breast and his face glistened in the light; his sarong, soaked, clung about his legs; he had his sheathed kriss in his left hand; and wisps of wet hair, escaping from under his red kerchief, stuck over his eyes and down his cheeks. He stepped in with a headlong stride and looking over his shoulder like a man pursued. Hollis turned on his side quickly and opened his eyes. Jackson clapped his big hand over the strings and the jingling vibration died suddenly. I stood up.

"We did not hear your boat's hail!" I exclaimed.

"Boat! The man's swum off," drawled out Hollis from the locker. "Look at him!"

He breathed heavily, wild-eyed, while we looked at him in silence. Water dripped from him, made a dark pool, and ran crookedly across the cabin floor. We could hear Jackson, who had gone out to drive away our Malay seamen from the doorway of the companion; he swore menacingly in the patter of a heavy shower, and there was a great commotion on deck. The watchmen, scared out of their wits by the glimpse of a shadowy figure leaping over the rail, straight out of the night as it were, had alarmed all hands.

Then Jackson, with glittering drops of water on his hair and beard, came back looking angry, and Hollis, who, being the youngest of us, assumed an indolent superiority, said without stirring, "Give him a dry sarong—give him mine; it's hanging up in the bathroom." Karain laid the kriss on the table, hilt inwards, and murmured a few words in a strangled voice.

"What's that?" asked Hollis, who had not heard.

"He apologizes for coming in with a weapon in his hand," I said, dazedly.

"Ceremonious beggar. Tell him we forgive a friend . . . on such a night," drawled out Hollis. "What's wrong?"

Karain slipped the dry sarong over his head, dropped the wet one at his feet, and stepped out of it. I pointed to the wooden armchair—his armchair. He sat down very straight, said "Ha!" in a strong voice; a short shiver shook his broad frame. He looked over his shoulder uneasily, turned as if to speak to us, but only stared in a curious blind manner, and again

looked back. Jackson bellowed out, "Watch well
on deck there!" heard a faint answer from above, and
reaching out with his foot slammed-to the cabin door.
"All right now," he said.

Karain's lips moved slightly. A vivid flash of
lightning made the two round sternports facing him
glimmer like a pair of cruel and phosphorescent eyes.
The flame of the lamp seemed to wither into brown
dust for an instant, and the looking-glass over the
little sideboard leaped out behind his back in a smooth
sheet of livid light. The roll of thunder came near,
crashed over us; the schooner trembled, and the great
voice went on, threatening terribly, into the distance.
For less than a minute a furious shower rattled on
the decks. Karain looked slowly from face to face,
and then the silence became so profound that we all
could hear distinctly the two chronometers in my cabin
ticking along with unflagging speed against one another.

And we three, strangely moved, could not take our
eyes from him. He had become enigmatical and touching, in virtue of that mysterious cause that had driven
him through the night and through the thunderstorm
to the shelter of the schooner's cuddy. Not one of us
doubted that we were looking at a fugitive, incredible
as it appeared to us. He was haggard, as though he
had not slept for weeks; he had become lean, as though
he had not eaten for days. His cheeks were hollow,
his eyes sunk, the muscles of his chest and arms twitched
slightly as if after an exhausting contest. Of course
it had been a long swim off to the schooner; but his
face showed another kind of fatigue, the tormented
weariness, the anger and the fear of a struggle against
a thought, an idea—against something that cannot
be grappled, that never rests—a shadow, a nothing,
unconquerable and immortal, that preys upon life.

We knew it as though he had shouted it at us. His chest expanded time after time, as if it could not contain the beating of his heart. For a moment he had the power of the possessed—the power to awaken in the beholders wonder, pain, pity, and a fearful near sense of things invisible, of things dark and mute, that surround the loneliness of mankind. His eyes roamed about aimlessly for a moment, then became still. He said with effort—

"I came here . . . I leaped out of my stockade as after a defeat. I ran in the night. The water was black. I left him calling on the edge of black water. . . . I left him standing alone on the beach. I swam . . . he called out after me . . . I swam . . ."

He trembled from head to foot, sitting very upright and gazing straight before him. Left whom? Who called? We did not know. We could not understand. I said at all hazards—

"Be firm."

The sound of my voice seemed to steady him into a sudden rigidity, but otherwise he took no notice. He seemed to listen, to expect something for a moment, then went on—

"He cannot come here—therefore I sought you. You men with white faces who despise the invisible voices. He cannot abide your unbelief and your strength."

He was silent for a while, then exclaimed softly—

"Oh! the strength of unbelievers!"

"There's no one here but you—and we three," said Hollis, quietly. He reclined with his head supported on elbow and did not budge.

"I know," said Karain. "He has never followed me here. Was not the wise man ever by my side?

But since the old wise man, who knew of my trouble, has died, I have heard the voice every night. I shut myself up—for many days—in the dark. I can hear the sorrowful murmurs of women, the whisper of the wind, of the running waters; the clash of weapons in the hands of faithful men, their footsteps—and his voice! . . . Near . . . So! In my ear! I felt him near . . . His breath passed over my neck. I leaped out without a cry. All about me men slept quietly. I ran to the sea. He ran by my side without footsteps, whispering, whispering old words—whispering into my ear in his old voice. I ran into the sea; I swam off to you, with my kriss between my teeth. I, armed, I fled before a breath—to you. Take me away to your land. The wise old man has died, and with him is gone the power of his words and charms. And I can tell no one. No one. There is no one here faithful enough and wise enough to know. It is only near you, unbelievers, that my trouble fades like a mist under the eye of day."

He turned to me.

"With you I go!" he cried in a contained voice. "With you, who know so many of us. I want to leave this land—my people . . . and him—there!"

He pointed a shaking finger at random over his shoulder. It was hard for us to bear the intensity of that undisclosed distress. Hollis stared at him hard. I asked gently—

"Where is the danger?"

"Everywhere outside this place," he answered, mournfully. "In every place where I am. He waits for me on the paths, under the trees, in the place where I sleep—everywhere but here."

He looked round the little cabin, at the painted beams, at the tarnished varnish of bulkheads; he looked round as if appealing to all its shabby strangeness, to the disorderly jumble of unfamiliar things that belong to an inconceivable life of stress, of power, of endeavour, of unbelief—to the strong life of white men, which rolls on irresistible and hard on the edge of outer darkness. He stretched out his arms as if to embrace it and us. We waited. The wind and rain had ceased, and the stillness of the night round the schooner was as dumb and complete as if a dead world had been laid to rest in a grave of clouds. We expected him to speak. The necessity within him tore at his lips. There are those who say that a native will not speak to a white man. Error. No man will speak to his master; but to a wanderer and a friend, to him who does not come to teach or to rule, to him who asks for nothing and accepts all things, words are spoken by the camp-fires, in the shared solitude of the sea, in riverside villages, in resting-places surrounded by forests—words are spoken that take no account of race or colour. One heart speaks—another one listens; and the earth, the sea, the sky, the passing wind and the stirring leaf, hear also the futile tale of the burden of life.

He spoke at last. It is impossible to convey the effect of his story. It is undying, it is but a memory, and its vividness cannot be made clear to another mind, any more than the vivid emotions of a dream. One must have seen his innate splendour, one must have known him before—looked at him then. The wavering gloom of the little cabin; the breathless stillness outside, through which only the lapping of water against the schooner's sides could be heard; Hollis's pale face, with steady dark eyes; the energetic head of Jackson held up between two big palms, and with the long yellow hair of his beard flowing over the strings of the guitar lying on the table; Karain's upright and motionless pose, his tone—all this made an impression that cannot be forgotten. He faced us across the table. His dark head and bronze torso appeared above the tarnished slab of wood, gleaming and still as if cast in metal. Only his lips moved, and his eyes glowed, went out, blazed again, or stared mournfully. His expressions came straight from his tormented heart. His words sounded low, in a sad murmur as of running water; at times they rang loud like the clash of a war-gong—or trailed slowly like weary travellers—or rushed forward with the speed of fear.

IV

This is, imperfectly, what he said—

"It was after the great trouble that broke the alliance of the four states of Wajo. We fought amongst ourselves, and the Dutch watched from afar till we were weary. Then the smoke of their fire-ships was seen at the mouth of our rivers, and their great men came in boats full of soldiers to talk to us of protection and peace. We answered with caution and wisdom, for our villages were burnt, our stockades weak, the people weary, and the weapons blunt. They came and went; there had been much talk, but after they went away everything seemed to be as before, only their ships remained in sight from our coast, and very soon their traders came amongst us under a promise of safety. My brother was a Ruler, and one of those who had given the promise. I was young then, and had fought in the war, and Pata Matara had fought by my side. We had shared hunger, danger, fatigue, and victory. His eyes saw my danger quickly, and twice my arm had preserved his life. It was his destiny. He was my friend. And he was great amongst us—one of those who were near my brother, the Ruler. He spoke in council, his courage was great, he was the chief of many villages round the great lake that is in the middle of our country as the heart is in the middle of a man's body. When his sword was carried into a campong in advance of his coming, the maidens whispered wonderingly under the fruit-trees, the rich men consulted together in the shade, and a feast was made ready with rejoicing and songs. He had the favour of the Ruler and the affection of the poor. He loved war, deer hunts, and the charms of women. He was the possessor of jewels, of lucky weapons, and of men's devotion. He was a fierce man; and I had no other friend.

"I was the chief of a stockade at the mouth of the river, and collected tolls for my brother from the passing boats. One day I saw a Dutch trader go up the river. He went up with three boats, and no toll was demanded from him, because the smoke of Dutch war-ships stood out from the open sea, and we were too weak to forget treaties. He went up under the promise of safety, and my brother gave him protection. He said he came to trade. He listened to our voices, for we are men who speak openly and without fear; he counted the number of our spears, he examined the trees, the running waters, the grasses of the bank, the slopes of our hills. He went up to Matara's country and obtained permission to build a house. He traded and planted. He despised our joys, our thoughts, and our sorrows. His face was red, his hair like flame, and his eyes pale, like a river mist; he moved heavily, and spoke with a deep voice; he laughed aloud like a fool, and knew no courtesy in his speech. He was a big, scornful man, who looked into women's faces and put his hand on the shoulders of free men as though he had been a noble-born chief. We bore with him. Time passed.

"Then Pata Matara's sister fled from the campong and went to live in the Dutchman's house. She was a great and wilful lady: I had seen her once carried high on slaves' shoulders amongst the people, with uncovered face, and I had heard all men say that her beauty was extreme, silencing the reason and ravishing the heart of the beholders. The people were dismayed; Matara's face was blackened with that disgrace, for she knew she had been promised to another man. Matara went to the Dutchman's house, and said, 'Give her up to die—she is the daughter of chiefs.' The white man refused and shut himself up, while his servants kept guard night and day with loaded guns. Matara raged. My brother called a council. But the Dutch ships were near, and watched our coast greedily. My brother said, 'If he dies now our land will pay for his blood. Leave him alone till we grow stronger and the ships are gone.' Matara was wise; he waited and watched. But the white man feared for her life and went away.

"He left his house, his plantations, and his goods! He departed, armed and menacing, and left all—for her! She had ravished his heart! From my stockade I saw him put out to sea in a big boat. Matara and I watched him from the fighting platform behind the pointed stakes. He sat cross-legged, with his gun in his hands, on the roof at the stern of his prau. The barrel of his rifle glinted aslant before his big red face. The broad river was stretched under him—level, smooth, shining, like a plain of silver; and his prau, looking very short and black from the shore, glided along the silver plain and over into the blue of the sea.

"Thrice Matara, standing by my side, called aloud her name with grief and imprecations. He stirred my heart. It leaped three times; and three times with the eye of my mind I saw in the gloom within the enclosed space of the prau a woman with streaming hair going away from her land and her people. I was angry—and sorry. Why? And then I also cried out insults and threats. Matara said, 'Now they have left our land their lives are mine. I shall follow and strike —and, alone, pay the price of blood.' A great wind was sweeping towards the setting sun over the empty river. I cried, 'By your side I will go!' He lowered his head in sign of assent. It was his destiny. The sun had set, and the trees swayed their boughs with a great noise above our heads.

"On the third night we two left our land together in a trading prau.

"The sea met us—the sea, wide, pathless, and without voice. A sailing prau leaves no track. We went south. The moon was full; and, looking up, we said to one another, 'When the next moon shines as this one, we shall return and they will be dead.' It was fifteen years ago. Many moons have grown full and withered and I have not seen my land since. We sailed south; we overtook many praus; we examined the creeks and the bays; we saw the end of our coast, of our island— a steep cape over a disturbed strait, where drift the shadows of shipwrecked praus and drowned men clamour in the night. The wide sea was all round us now. We saw a great mountain burning in the midst of water; we saw thousands of islets scattered like bits of iron fired from a big gun; we saw a long coast of mountain and lowlands stretching away in sunshine from west to east. It was Java. We said, 'They are there; their time is near, and we shall return or die cleansed from dishonour.'

"We landed. Is there anything good in that country? The paths run straight and hard and dusty. Stone campongs, full of white faces, are surrounded by fertile fields, but every man you meet is a slave. The rulers live under the edge of a foreign sword. We ascended mountains, we traversed valleys; at sunset we entered villages. We asked everyone, 'Have you

seen such a white man?' Some stared; others laughed;
women gave us food, sometimes, with fear and respect,
as though we had been distracted by the visitation of
God; but some did not understand our language, and
some cursed us, or, yawning, asked with contempt
the reason of our quest. Once, as we were going
away, an old man called after us, 'Desist!'

"We went on. Concealing our weapons, we stood
humbly aside before the horsemen on the road; we
bowed low in the courtyards of chiefs who were no
better than slaves. We lost ourselves in the fields,
in the jungle; and one night, in a tangled forest, we
came upon a place where crumbling old walls had
fallen amongst the trees, and where strange stone
idols—carved images of devils with many arms and
legs, with snakes twined round their bodies, with
twenty heads and holding a hundred swords—seemed
to live and threaten in the light of our camp fire.
Nothing dismayed us. And on the road, by every fire,
in resting-places, we always talked of her and of him.
Their time was near. We spoke of nothing else. No!
not of hunger, thirst, weariness, and faltering hearts.
No! we spoke of him and her! Of her! And we
thought of them—of her! Matara brooded by the fire.
I sat and thought and thought, till suddenly I could
see again the image of a woman, beautiful, and young,
and great and proud, and tender, going away from her
land and her people. Matara said, 'When we find
them we shall kill her first to cleanse the dishonour—
then the man must die.' I would say, 'It shall be so;
it is your vengeance.' He stared long at me with his
big sunken eyes.

"We came back to the coast. Our feet were bleeding, our bodies thin. We slept in rags under the shadow
of stone enclosures; we prowled, soiled and lean, about

the gateways of white men's courtyards. Their hairy dogs barked at us, and their servants shouted from afar, 'Begone!' Low-born wretches, that keep watch over the streets of stone campongs, asked us who we were. We lied, we cringed, we smiled with hate in our hearts, and we kept looking here, looking there for them—for the white man with hair like flame, and for her, for the woman who had broken faith, and therefore must die. We looked. At last in every woman's face I thought I could see hers. We ran swiftly. No! Sometimes Matara would whisper, 'Here is the man,' and we waited, crouching. He came near. It was not the man—those Dutchmen are all alike. We suffered the anguish of deception. In my sleep I saw her face, and was both joyful and sorry. . . . Why? . . . I seemed to hear a whisper near me. I turned swiftly. She was not there! And as we trudged wearily from stone city to stone city I seemed to hear a light footstep near me. A time came when I heard it always, and I was glad. I thought, walking dizzy and weary in sunshine on the hard paths of white men—I thought, She is there—with us! . . . Matara was sombre. We were often hungry.

"We sold the carved sheaths of our krisses—the ivory sheaths with golden ferules. We sold the jewelled hilts. But we kept the blades—for them. The blades that never touch but kill—we kept the blades for her. . . . Why? She was always by our side. . . . We starved. We begged. We left Java at last.

"We went West, we went East. We saw many lands, crowds of strange faces, men that live in trees and men who eat their old people. We cut rattans in the forest for a handful of rice, and for a living swept the decks of big ships and heard curses heaped upon our heads. We toiled in villages; we wandered upon the seas with the Bajow people, who have no country. We fought for pay; we hired ourselves to work for Goram men, and were cheated; and under the orders of rough white faces we dived for pearls in barren bays, dotted with black rocks, upon a coast of sand and desolation. And everywhere we watched, we listened, we asked. We asked traders, robbers, white men. We heard jeers, mockery, threats—words of wonder and words of contempt. We never knew rest; we never thought of home, for our work was not done. A year passed, then another. I ceased to count the number of nights, of moons, of years. I watched over Matara. He had my last handful of rice; if there was water enough for one he drank it; I covered him up when he shivered with cold; and when the hot sickness came upon him I sat sleepless through many nights and fanned his face. He was a fierce man, and my friend. He spoke of her with fury in the daytime, with sorrow in the dark; he remembered her in health, in sickness. I said nothing; but I saw her every day—always! At first I saw only her head, as of a woman walking in the low mist on a river bank. Then she sat by our fire. I saw her! I looked at her! She had tender eyes and a ravishing face. I murmured to her in the night. Matara said sleepily sometimes, 'To whom are you talking? Who is there?' I answered quickly, 'No one' . . . It was a lie! She never left me. She shared the warmth of our fire, she sat on my couch of leaves, she swam on the sea to follow me. . . . I saw her! . . . I tell you I saw her long black hair spread behind her upon the moonlit water as she struck out with bare arms by the side of a swift prau. She was beautiful, she was faithful, and in the silence

of foreign countries she spoke to me very low in the
language of my people. No one saw her; no one heard
her; she was mine only! In daylight she moved with
a swaying walk before me upon the weary paths; her
figure was straight and flexible like the stem of a slender
tree; the heels of her feet were round and polished like
shells of eggs; with her round arm she made signs.
At night she looked into my face. And she was sad!
Her eyes were tender and frightened; her voice soft
and pleading. Once I murmured to her, 'You shall not
die,' and she smiled . . . ever after she smiled! . . .
She gave me courage to bear weariness and hardships.
Those were times of pain, and she soothed me. We
wandered patient in our search. We knew deception,
false hopes; we knew captivity, sickness, thirst, misery,
despair . . . . Enough! We found them! . . ."

He cried out the last words and paused. His face
was impassive, and he kept still like a man in a trance.
Hollis sat up quickly, and spread his elbows on the
table. Jackson made a brusque movement, and ac-
cidentally touched the guitar. A plaintive resonance
filled the cabin with confused vibrations and died out
slowly. Then Karain began to speak again. The restrained fierceness of his tone seemed to rise like a
voice from outside, like a thing unspoken but heard;
it filled the cabin and enveloped in its intense and
deadened murmur the motionless figure in the chair.

"We were on our way to Atjeh, where there was
war; but the vessel ran on a sandbank, and we had to
land in Delli. We had earned a little money, and
had bought a gun from some Selangore traders; only
one gun, which was fired by the spark of a stone:
Matara carried it. We landed. Many white men
lived there, planting tobacco on conquered plains,
and Matara . . . But no matter. He saw him!

. . . The Dutchman! . . . At last! . . .
We crept and watched. Two nights and a day we
watched. He had a house—a big house in a clearing in the midst of his fields; flowers and bushes grew
around; there were narrow paths of yellow earth between the cut grass, and thick hedges to keep people
out. The third night we came armed, and lay behind
a hedge.

"A heavy dew seemed to soak through our flesh
and made our very entrails cold. The grass, the twigs,
the leaves, covered with drops of water, were gray
in the moonlight. Matara, curled up in the grass,
shivered in his sleep. My teeth rattled in my head
so loud that I was afraid the noise would wake up all
the land. Afar, the watchmen of white men's houses
struck wooden clappers and hooted in the darkness.
And, as every night, I saw her by my side. She
smiled no more! . . . The fire of anguish burned in
my breast, and she whispered to me with compassion,
with pity, softly—as women will; she soothed the pain
of my mind; she bent her face over me—the face of a
woman who ravishes the hearts and silences the reason
of men. She was all mine, and no one could see her—
no one of living mankind! Stars shone through her
bosom, through her floating hair. I was overcome
with regret, with tenderness, with sorrow. Matara
slept . . . Had I slept? Matara was shaking me
by the shoulder, and the fire of the sun was drying the
grass, the bushes, the leaves. It was day. Shreds of
white mist hung between the branches of trees.

"Was it night or day? I saw nothing again till I
heard Matara breathe quickly where he lay, and then
outside the house I saw her. I saw them both. They
had come out. She sat on a bench under the wall, and
twigs laden with flowers crept high above her head, hung

over her hair. She had a box on her lap, and gazed into it, counting the increase of her pearls. The Dutchman stood by looking on; he smiled down at her; his white teeth flashed; the hair on his lip was like two twisted flames. He was big and fat, and joyous, and without fear. Matara tipped fresh priming from the hollow of his palm, scraped the flint with his thumb-nail, and gave the gun to me. To me! I took it . . . O fate!

"He whispered into my ear, lying on his stomach, 'I shall creep close and then amok . . . let her die by my hand. You take aim at the fat swine there. Let him see me strike my shame off the face of the earth— and then . . . you are my friend—kill with a sure shot.' I said nothing; there was no air in my chest—there was no air in the world. Matara had gone suddenly from my side. The grass nodded. Then a bush rustled. She lifted her head.

"I saw her! The consoler of sleepless nights, of weary days; the companion of troubled years! I saw her! She looked straight at the place where I crouched. She was there as I had seen her for years—a faithful wanderer by my side. She looked with sad eyes and had smiling lips; she looked at me . . . Smiling lips! Had I not promised that she should not die!

"She was far off and I felt her near. Her touch caressed me, and her voice murmured, whispered above me, around me, 'Who shall be thy companion, who shall console thee if I die?' I saw a flowering thicket to the left of her stir a little . . . Matara was ready . . . I cried aloud—'Return!'

"She leaped up; the box fell; the pearls streamed at her feet. The big Dutchman by her side rolled menacing eyes through the still sunshine. The gun went up to my shoulder. I was kneeling and I was firm—

firmer than the trees, the rocks, the mountains. But in front of the steady long barrel the fields, the house, the earth, the sky swayed to and fro like shadows in a forest on a windy day. Matara burst out of the thicket; before him the petals of torn flowers whirled high as if driven by a tempest. I heard her cry; I saw her spring with open arms in front of the white man. She was a woman of my country and of noble blood. They are so! I heard her shriek of anguish and fear— and all stood still! The fields, the house, the earth, the sky stood still—while Matara leaped at her with uplifted arm. I pulled the trigger, saw a spark, heard nothing; the smoke drove back into my face, and then I could see Matara roll over head first and lie with stretched arms at her feet. Ha! A sure shot! The sunshine fell on my back colder than the running water. A sure shot! I flung the gun after the shot. Those two stood over the dead man as though they had been bewitched by a charm. I shouted at her, 'Live and remember!' Then for a time I stumbled about in a cold darkness.

"Behind me there were great shouts, the running of many feet; strange men surrounded me, cried meaningless words into my face, pushed me, dragged me, supported me . . . I stood before the big Dutchman: he stared as if bereft of his reason. He wanted to know, he talked fast, he spoke of gratitude, he offered me food, shelter, gold—he asked many questions. I laughed in his face. I said, 'I am a Korinchi traveller from Perak over there, and know nothing of that dead man. I was passing along the path when I heard a shot, and your senseless people rushed out and dragged me here.' He lifted his arms, he wondered, he could not believe, he could not understand, he clamoured in his own tongue! She had her arms clasped round his neck, and over her shoulder stared back at me with wide eyes. I smiled and looked at her; I smiled and waited to hear the sound of her voice. The white man asked her suddenly, 'Do you know him?' I listened—my life was in my ears! She looked at me long, she looked at me with unflinching eyes, and said aloud, 'No! I never saw him before.' . . . What! Never before? Had she forgotten already? Was it possible? Forgotten already—after so many years—so many years of wandering, of companionship, of trouble, of tender words! Forgotten already! . . . I tore myself out from the hands that held me and went away without a word . . . They let me go.

"I was weary. Did I sleep? I do not know. I remember walking upon a broad path under a clear starlight; and that strange country seemed so big, the rice-fields so vast, that, as I looked around, my head swam with the fear of space. Then I saw a forest. The joyous starlight was heavy upon me. I turned off the path and entered the forest, which was very sombre and very sad."

V

KARAIN's tone had been getting lower and lower, as though he had been going away from us, till the last words sounded faint but clear, as if shouted on a calm day from a very great distance. He moved not. He stared fixedly past the motionless head of Hollis, who faced him, as still as himself. Jackson had turned sideways, and with elbow on the table shaded his eyes with the palm of his hand. And I looked on, surprised and moved; I looked at that man, loyal to a vision, betrayed by his dream, spurned by his illusion, and coming to us unbelievers for help—against a thought. The silence was profound; but it seemed full of noiseless phantoms, of things sorrowful, shadowy, and mute, in whose invisible presence the firm, pulsating beat of the two ship's chronometers ticking off steadily the seconds of Greenwich Time seemed to me a protection and a relief. Karain stared stonily; and looking at his rigid figure, I thought of his wanderings, of that obscure Odyssey of revenge, of all the men that wander amongst illusions; of the illusions as restless as men; of the illusions faithful, faithless; of the illusions that give joy, that give sorrow, that give pain, that give peace; of the invincible illusions that can make life and death appear serene, inspiring, tormented, or ignoble.

A murmur was heard; that voice from outside seemed to flow out of a dreaming world into the lamplight of the cabin. Karain was speaking.

"I lived in the forest.

40

"She came no more. Never! Never once! I lived alone. She had forgotten. It was well. I did not want her; I wanted no one. I found an abandoned house in an old clearing. Nobody came near. Sometimes I heard in the distance the voices of people going along a path. I slept; I rested; there was wild rice, water from a running stream—and peace! Every night I sat alone by my small fire before the hut. Many nights passed over my head.

"Then, one evening, as I sat by my fire after having eaten, I looked down on the ground and began to remember my wanderings. I lifted my head. I had heard no sound, no rustle, no footsteps—but I lifted my head. A man was coming towards me across the small clearing. I waited. He came up without a greeting and squatted down into the firelight. Then he turned his face to me. It was Matara. He stared at me fiercely with his big sunken eyes. The night was cold; the heat died suddenly out of the fire, and he stared at me. I rose and went away from there, leaving him by the fire that had no heat.

"I walked all that night, all next day, and in the evening made up a big blaze and sat down—to wait for him. He had not come into the light. I heard him in the bushes here and there, whispering, whispering. I understood at last—I had heard the words before, 'You are my friend—kill with a sure shot.'

"I bore it as long as I could—then leaped away, as on this very night I leaped from my stockade and swam to you. I ran—I ran crying like a child left alone and far from the houses. He ran by my side, without footsteps, whispering, whispering—invisible and heard. I sought people—I wanted men around me! Men who had not died! And again we two wandered. I sought danger, violence, and death. I fought in the Atjeh war, and a brave people wondered at the valiance of a stranger. But we were two; he warded off the blows . . . Why? I wanted peace, not life. And no one could see him; no one knew— I dared tell no one. At times he would leave me, but not for long; then he would return and whisper or stare. My heart was torn with a strange fear, but could not die. Then I met an old man.

"You all knew him. People here called him my sorcerer, my servant and sword-bearer; but to me he was father, mother, protection, refuge and peace. When I met him he was returning from a pilgrimage, and I heard him intoning the prayer of sunset. He had gone to the holy place with his son, his son's wife, and a little child; and on their return, by the favour of the Most High, they all died: the strong man, the young mother, the little child—they died; and the old man reached his country alone. He was a pilgrim serene and pious, very wise and very lonely. I told him all. For a time we lived together. He said over me words of compassion, of wisdom, of prayer. He warded from me the shade of the dead. I begged him for a charm that would make me safe. For a long time he refused; but at last, with a sigh and a smile, he gave me one. Doubtless he could command a spirit stronger than the unrest of my dead friend, and again I had peace; but I had become restless, and a lover of turmoil and danger. The old man never left me. We travelled together. We were welcomed by the great; his wisdom and my courage are remembered where your strength, O white men, is forgotten! We served the Sultan of Sula. We fought the Spaniards. There were victories, hopes, defeats, sorrow, blood, women's tears . . . What for? . . . We fled. We collected wanderers of a warlike race and came here to fight again. The rest you know. I am the ruler of a conquered land, a lover of war and danger, a fighter and a plotter. But the old man has died, and I am again the slave of the dead. He is not here now to drive away the reproachful shade—to silence the lifeless voice! The power of his charm has died with him. And I know fear; and I hear the whisper, 'Kill! kill! kill!' . . . Have I not killed enough? . . ."

For the first time that night a sudden convulsion of madness and rage passed over his face. His wavering glances darted here and there like scared birds in a thunderstorm. He jumped up, shouting—

"By the spirits that drink blood: by the spirits that cry in the night: by all the spirits of fury, misfortune, and death, I swear—some day I will strike into every heart I meet—I . . ."

He looked so dangerous that we all three leaped to our feet, and Hollis, with the back of his hand, sent the kriss flying off the table. I believe we shouted together. It was a short scare, and the next moment he was again composed in his chair, with three white men standing over him in rather foolish attitudes. We felt a little ashamed of ourselves. Jackson picked up the kriss, and, after an inquiring glance at me, gave it to him. He received it with a stately inclination of the head and stuck it in the twist of his sarong, with punctilious care to give his weapon a pacific position. Then he looked up at us with an austere smile. We were abashed and reproved. Hollis sat sideways on the table and, holding his chin in his hand, scrutinized him in pensive silence. I said—

"You must abide with your people. They need you. And there is forgetfulness in life. Even the dead cease to speak in time."

"Am I a woman, to forget long years before an

eyelid has had the time to beat twice?" he exclaimed, with bitter resentment. He startled me. It was amazing. To him his life—that cruel mirage of love and peace—seemed as real, as undeniable, as theirs would be to any saint, philosopher, or fool of us all. Hollis muttered—

"You won't soothe him with your platitudes."

Karain spoke to me.

"You know us. You have lived with us. Why?— we cannot know; but you understand our sorrows and our thoughts. You have lived with my people, and you understand our desires and our fears. With you I will go. To your land—to your people. To your people, who live in unbelief; to whom day is day, and night is night—nothing more, because you understand all things seen, and despise all else! To your land of unbelief, where the dead do not speak, where every man is wise, and alone—and at peace!"

"Capital description," murmured Hollis, with the flicker of a smile.

Karain hung his head.

"I can toil, and fight—and be faithful," he whispered, in a weary tone, "but I cannot go back to him who waits for me on the shore. No! Take me with you . . . Or else give me some of your strength—of your unbelief . . . A charm! . . ."

He seemed utterly exhausted.

"Yes, take him home," said Hollis, very low, as if debating with himself. "That would be one way. The ghosts there are in society, and talk affably to ladies and gentlemen, but would scorn a naked human being— like our princely friend. . . . Naked . . . Flayed! I should say. I am sorry for him. Impossible—of course. The end of all this shall be," he went on, looking up at us—"the end of this shall be, that some

ay he will run amuck amongst his faithful subjects
nd send *ad patres* ever so many of them before they
ake up their minds to the disloyalty of knocking
im on the head."

I nodded. I thought it more than probable that
ach would be the end of Karain. It was evident that
e had been hunted by his thought along the very
mit of human endurance, and very little more pressing
as needed to make him swerve over into the form of
adness peculiar to his race. The respite he had
uring the old man's life made the return of the tor-
ent unbearable. That much was clear.

He lifted his head suddenly; we had imagined for a
oment that he had been dozing.

"Give me your protection—or your strength!" he
ried. "A charm . . . a weapon!"

Again his chin fell on his breast. We looked at him,
hen looked at one another with suspicious awe in our
yes, like men who come unexpectedly upon the scene
f some mysterious disaster. He had given himself
p to us; he had thrust into our hands his errors and
is torment, his life and his peace; and we did not know
vhat to do with that problem from the outer darkness.
Ve three white men, looking at the Malay, could not
ind one word to the purpose amongst us—if indeed
here existed a word that could solve that problem.
Ve pondered, and our hearts sank. We felt as though
ve three had been called to the very gate of Infernal
Regions to judge, to decide the fate of a wanderer
:oming suddenly from a world of sunshine and illusions.

"By Jove, he seems to have a great idea of our power,"
whispered Hollis, hopelessly. And then again there
was a silence, the feeble plash of water, the steady tick
of chronometers. Jackson, with bare arms crossed,
leaned his shoulders against the bulkhead of the cabin.

He was bending his head under the deck beam; his
fair beard spread out magnificently over his chest;
he looked colossal, ineffectual, and mild. There was
something lugubrious in the aspect of the cabin; the
air in it seemed to become slowly charged with the
cruel chill of helplessness, with the pitiless anger of
egoism against the incomprehensible form of an intruding pain. We had no idea what to do; we began to
resent bitterly the hard necessity to get rid of him.

Hollis mused, muttered suddenly with a short laugh,
"Strength . . . Protection . . . Charm." He slipped
off the table and left the cuddy without a look at us.
It seemed a base desertion. Jackson and I exchanged
indignant glances. We could hear him rummaging
in his pigeon-hole of a cabin. Was the fellow actually
going to bed? Karain sighed. It was intolerable!

Then Hollis reappeared, holding in both hands a
small leather box. He put it down gently on the table
and looked at us with a queer gasp, we thought, as
though he had from some cause become speechless
for a moment, or were ethically uncertain about pro-
ducing that box. But in an instant the insolent and
unerring wisdom of his youth gave him the needed
courage. He said, as he unlocked the box with a very
small key, "Look as solemn as you can, you fellows."

Probably we looked only surprised and stupid, for
he glanced over his shoulder, and said angrily—

"This is no play; I am going to do something for
him. Look serious. Confound it! . . . Can't you
lie a little . . . for a friend!"

Karain seemed to take no notice of us, but when Hollis
threw open the lid of the box his eyes flew to it—and so
did ours. The quilted crimson satin of the inside put
a violent patch of colour into the sombre atmosphere; it
was something positive to look at—it was fascinating.

VI

HOLLIS looked smiling into the box. He had lately
made a dash home through the Canal. He had been
away six months, and only joined us again just in time
for this last trip. We had never seen the box before.
His hands hovered above it; and he talked to us ironi-
cally, but his face became as grave as though he were
pronouncing a powerful incantation over the things
inside.

"Every one of us," he said, with pauses that somehow were more offensive than his words—"every one
of us, you'll admit, has been haunted by some woman
. . And . . . as to friends . . . dropped
by the way . . . Well! . . . ask yourselves . . ."

He paused. Karain stared. A deep rumble was
heard high up under the deck. Jackson spoke seriously—

"Don't be so beastly cynical."

"Ah! You are without guile," said Hollis, sadly.
"You will learn . . . Meantime this Malay has been
our friend . . ."

He repeated several times thoughtfully, "Friend . . .
Malay. Friend, Malay," as though weighing the
words against one another, then went on more briskly—

"A good fellow—a gentleman in his way. We can't,
so to speak, turn our backs on his confidence and belief in us. Those Malays are easily impressed—all
nerves, you know—therefore . . ."

He turned to me sharply.

"You know him best," he said, in a practical tone. "Do you think he is fanatical—I mean very strict in his faith?"

I stammered in profound amazement that "I did not think so."

"It's on account of its being a likeness—an engraved image," muttered Hollis, enigmatically, turning to the box. He plunged his fingers into it. Karain's lips were parted and his eyes shone. We looked into the box.

There were there a couple of reels of cotton, a packet of needles, a bit of silk ribbon, dark blue; a cabinet photograph, at which Hollis stole a glance before laying it on the table face downwards. A girl's portrait, I could see. There were, amongst a lot of various small objects, a bunch of flowers, a narrow white glove with many buttons, a slim packet of letters carefully tied up. Amulets of white men! Charms and talismans! Charms that keep them straight, that drive them crooked, that have the power to make a young man sigh, an old man smile. Potent things that procure dreams of joy, thoughts of regret; that soften hard hearts, and can temper a soft one to the hardness of steel. Gifts of heaven—things of earth . . .

Hollis rummaged in the box.

And it seemed to me, during that moment of waiting, that the cabin of the schooner was becoming filled with a stir invisible and living as of subtle breaths. All the ghosts driven out of the unbelieving West by men who pretend to be wise and alone and at peace—all the homeless ghosts of an unbelieving world—appeared suddenly round the figure of Hollis bending over the box; all the exiled and charming shades of loved women; all the beautiful and tender ghosts of ideals, remembered, forgotten, cherished, execrated,

ll the cast-out and reproachful ghosts of friends
dmired, trusted, traduced, betrayed, left dead by
he way—they all seemed to come from the inhospitable
egions of the earth to crowd into the gloomy cabin, as
hough it had been a refuge and, in all the unbelieving
vorld, the only place of avenging belief. . . . It lasted
second—all disappeared. Hollis was facing us alone
vith something small that glittered between his fingers.
t looked like a coin.

"Ah! here it is," he said.

He held it up. It was a sixpence—a Jubilee sixpence.
t was gilt; it had a hole punched near the rim. Hollis
ooked towards Karain.

"A charm for our friend," he said to us. "The
hing itself is of great power—money, you know—and
is imagination is struck. A loyal vagabond; if only
is puritanism doesn't shy at a likeness . . ."

We said nothing. We did not know whether to be
candalized, amused, or relieved. Hollis advanced
owards Karain, who stood up as if startled, and then,
olding the coin up, spoke in Malay.

"This is the image of the Great Queen, and the most
owerful thing the white men know," he said, solemnly.

Karain covered the handle of his kriss in sign of
espect, and stared at the crowned head.

"The Invincible, the Pious," he muttered.

"She is more powerful than Suleiman the Wise, who
ommanded the genii, as you know," said Hollis,
ravely. "I shall give this to you."

He held the sixpence in the palm of his hand, and
ooking at it thoughtfully, spoke to us in English.

"She commands a spirit, too—the spirit of her nation;
masterful, conscientious, unscrupulous, unconquer-
ble devil . . . that does a lot of good—incident-
lly . . . a lot of good . . . at times—and

wouldn't stand any fuss from the best ghost out for such a little thing as our friend's shot. Don't look thunderstruck, you fellows. Help me to make him believe—everything's in that."

"His people will be shocked," I murmured.

Hollis looked fixedly at Karain, who was the incarnation of the very essence of still excitement. He stood rigid, with head thrown back; his eyes rolled wildly, flashing; the dilated nostrils quivered.

"Hang it all!" said Hollis at last, "he is a good fellow I'll give him something that I shall really miss."

He took the ribbon out of the box, smiled at it scornfully, then with a pair of scissors cut out a piece from the palm of the glove.

"I shall make him a thing like those Italian peasant wear, you know."

He sewed the coin in the delicate leather, sewed the leather to the ribbon, tied the ends together. He worked with haste. Karain watched his fingers all the time.

"Now then," he said—then stepped up to Karain. They looked close into one another's eyes. Those of Karain stared in a lost glance, but Hollis's seemed to grow darker and looked out masterful and compelling. They were in violent contrast together—one motionless and the colour of bronze, the other dazzling white, and lifting his arms, where the powerful muscle rolled slightly under a skin that gleamed like satin. Jackson moved near with the air of a man closing up to a chum in a tight place. I said impressively, pointing to Hollis——

"He is young, but he is wise. Believe him!"

Karain bent his head: Hollis threw lightly over it the dark-blue ribbon and stepped back.

"Forget, and be at peace!" I cried.

Karain seemed to wake up from a dream. He said, "Ha!" shook himself as if throwing off a burden. He looked round with assurance. Someone on deck dragged off the skylight cover, and a flood of light fell into the cabin. It was morning already.

"Time to go on deck," said Jackson.

Hollis put on a coat, and we went up, Karain leading. The sun had risen beyond the hills, and their long shadows stretched far over the bay in the pearly light. The air was clear, stainless, and cool. I pointed at the curved line of yellow sands.

"He is not there," I said, emphatically, to Karain. "He waits no more. He has departed forever."

A shaft of bright hot rays darted into the bay between the summits of two hills, and the water all round broke out as if by magic into a dazzling sparkle.

"No! He is not there waiting," said Karain, after a long look over the beach. "I do not hear him," he went on, slowly. "No!"

He turned to us.

"He has departed again—forever!" he cried.

We assented vigorously, repeatedly, and without compunction. The great thing was to impress him powerfully; to suggest absolute safety—the end of all trouble. We did our best; and I hope we affirmed our faith in the power of Hollis's charm efficiently enough to put the matter beyond the shadow of a doubt. Our voices rang around him joyously in the still air, and above his head the sky, pellucid, pure, stainless, arched its tender blue from shore to shore and over the bay, as if to envelop the water, the earth, and the man in the caress of its light.

The anchor was up, the sails hung still, and half-a-dozen big boats were seen sweeping over the bay to give us a tow out. The paddlers in the first one that came alongside lifted their heads and saw their ruler standing amongst us. A low murmur of surprise arose —then a shout of greeting.

He left us, and seemed straightway to step into the glorious splendour of his stage, to wrap himself in the illusion of unavoidable success. For a moment he stood erect, one foot over the gangway, one hand on the hilt of his kriss, in a martial pose; and, relieved from the fear of outer darkness, he held his head high, he swept a serene look over his conquered foothold on the earth. The boats far off took up the cry of greeting; a great clamour rolled on the water; the hills echoed it, and seemed to toss back at him the words invoking long life and victories.

He descended into a canoe, and as soon as he was clear of the side we gave him three cheers. They sounded faint and orderly after the wild tumult of his loyal subjects, but it was the best we could do. He stood up in the boat, lifted up both his arms, then pointed to the infallible charm. We cheered again; and the Malays in the boats stared—very much puzzled and impressed. I wondered what they thought; what he thought; . . . what the reader thinks?

We towed out slowly. We saw him land and watch us from the beach. A figure approached him humbly but openly—not at all like a ghost with a grievance. We could see other men running towards him. Perhaps he had been missed? At any rate there was a great stir. A group formed itself rapidly near him, and he walked along the sands, followed by a growing *cortége* and kept nearly abreast of the schooner. With our glasses we could see the blue ribbon on his neck and a patch of white on his brown chest. The bay was waking up. The smokes of morning fires stood in faint spirals higher than the heads of palms; people

moved between the houses; a herd of buffaloes galloped
clumsily across a green slope; the slender figures of boys
brandishing sticks appeared black and leaping in the
long grass; a coloured line of women, with water bamboos on their heads, moved swaying through a thin
grove of fruit-trees. Karain stopped in the midst of
his men and waved his hand; then, detaching himself
from the splendid group, walked alone to the water's
edge and waved his hand again. The schooner passed
out to sea between the steep headlands that shut in the
bay, and at the same instant Karain passed out of our
life forever.

But the memory remains. Some years afterwards
I met Jackson, in the Strand. He was magnificent as
ever. His head was high above the crowd. His
beard was gold, his face red, his eyes blue; he had a
wide-brimmed gray hat and no collar or waistcoat;
he was inspiring; he had just come home—had landed
that very day! Our meeting caused an eddy in the
current of humanity. Hurried people would run
against us, then walk round us, and turn back to look
at that giant. We tried to compress seven years of
life into seven exclamations; then, suddenly appeased,
walked sedately along, giving one another the news of
yesterday. Jackson gazed about him, like a man who
looks for landmarks, then stopped before Bland's
window. He always had a passion for firearms; so he
stopped short and contemplated the row of weapons,
perfect and severe, drawn up in a line behind the black-
framed panes. I stood by his side. Suddenly he said—

"Do you remember Karain?"

I nodded.

"The sight of all this made me think of him," he went
on, with his face near the glass . . . and I could
see another man, powerful and bearded, peering at him

intently from amongst the dark and polished tubes that can cure so many illusions. "Yes; it made me think of him," he continued, slowly. "I saw a paper this morning; they are fighting over there again. He's sure to be in it. He will make it hot for the caballeros. Well, good luck to him, poor devil! He was perfectly stunning."

We walked on.

"I wonder whether the charm worked—you remember Hollis's charm, of course. If it did . . . never was a sixpence wasted to better advantage! Poor devil! I wonder whether he got rid of that friend of his. Hope so. . . . Do you know, I sometimes think that——"

I stood still and looked at him.

"Yes . . . I mean, whether the thing was so, you know . . . whether it really happened to him. . . . What do you think?"

"My dear chap," I cried, "you have been too long away from home. What a question to ask! Only look at all this."

A watery gleam of sunshine flashed from the west and went out between two long lines of walls; and then the broken confusion of roofs, the chimney-stacks, the gold letters sprawling over the fronts of houses, the sombre polish of windows, stood resigned and sullen under the falling gloom. The whole length of the street, deep as a well and narrow like a corridor, was full of a sombre and ceaseless stir. Our ears were filled by a headlong shuffle and beat of rapid footsteps and an underlying rumour—a rumour vast, faint, pulsating, as of panting breaths, of beating hearts, of gasping voices. Innumerable eyes stared straight in front, feet moved hurriedly, blank faces flowed, arms swung. Over all, a narrow ragged strip of smoky sky wound about between the high roofs, extended and motionless, like a soiled streamer flying above the rout of a mob.

"Ye-e-e-s," said Jackson, meditatively.

The big wheels of hansoms turned slowly along the edge of side-walks; a pale-faced youth strolled, overcome by weariness, by the side of his stick and with the tails of his overcoat flapping gently near his heels; horses stepped gingerly on the greasy pavement, tossing their heads; two young girls passed by, talking vivaciously and with shining eyes; a fine old fellow strutted, red-faced, stroking a white moustache; and a line of yellow boards with blue letters on them approached us slowly, tossing on high behind one another like some queer wreckage adrift upon a river of hats.

"Ye-e-es," repeated Jackson. His clear blue eyes looked about, contemptuous, amused and hard, like the eyes of a boy. A clumsy string of red, yellow, and green omnibuses rolled swaying, monstrous and gaudy; two shabby children ran across the road; a knot of dirty men with red neckerchiefs round their bare throats lurched along, discussing filthily; a ragged old man with a face of despair yelled horribly in the mud the name of a paper; while far off, amongst the tossing heads of horses, the dull flash of harnesses, the jumble of lustrous panels and roofs of carriages, we could see a policeman, helmeted and dark, stretching out a rigid arm at the crossing of the streets.

"Yes; I see it," said Jackson, slowly. "It is there; it pants, it runs, it rolls; it is strong and alive; it would smash you if you didn't look out; but I'll be hanged if it is yet as real to me as . . . as the other thing . . . say, Karain's story."

I think that, decidedly, he had been too long away from home.

THE IDIOTS

WE WERE driving along the road from Treguier to Kervanda. We passed at a smart trot between the hedges topping an earth wall on each side of the road; then at the foot of the steep ascent before Ploumar the horse dropped into a walk, and the driver jumped down heavily from the box. He flicked his whip and climbed the incline, stepping clumsily uphill by the side of the carriage, one hand on the footboard, his eyes on the ground. After a while he lifted his head, pointed up the road with the end of the whip, and said—

"The idiot!"

The sun was shining violently upon the undulating surface of the land. The rises were topped by clumps of meagre trees, with their branches showing high on the sky as if they had been perched upon stilts. The small fields, cut up by hedges and stone walls that zig-zagged over the slopes, lay in rectangular patches of vivid greens and yellows, resembling the unskilful daubs of a naïve picture. And the landscape was divided in two by the white streak of a road stretching in long loops far away, like a river of dust crawling out of the hills on its way to the sea.

"Here he is," said the driver, again.

In the long grass bordering the road a face glided past the carriage at the level of the wheels as we drove slowly by. The imbecile face was red, and the bullet head with close-cropped hair seemed to lie alone, its chin in the dust. The body was lost in the bushes growing thick along the bottom of the deep ditch.

It was a boy's face. He might have been sixteen, judging from the size—perhaps less, perhaps more. Such creatures are forgotten by time, and live untouched by years till death gathers them up into its compassionate bosom; the faithful death that never forgets in the press of work the most insignificant of its children.

"Ah! there's another," said the man, with a certain satisfaction in his tone, as if he had caught sight of something expected.

There was another. That one stood nearly in the middle of the road in the blaze of sunshine at the end of his own short shadow. And he stood with hands pushed into the opposite sleeves of his long coat, his head sunk between the shoulders, all hunched up in the flood of heat. From a distance he had the aspect of one suffering from intense cold.

"Those are twins," explained the driver.

The idiot shuffled two paces out of the way and looked at us over his shoulder when we brushed past him. The glance was unseeing and staring, a fascinated glance; but he did not turn to look after us. Probably the image passed before the eyes without leaving any trace on the misshapen brain of the creature. When we had topped the ascent I looked over the hood. He stood in the road just where we had left him.

The driver clambered into his seat, clicked his tongue, and we went downhill. The brake squeaked horribly from time to time. At the foot he eased off the noisy mechanism and said, turning half round on his box—

"We shall see some more of them by-and-by."

"More idiots? How many of them are there, then?" I asked.

"There's four of them—children of a farmer near

Ploumar here. . . . The parents are dead now," he
added, after a while. "The grandmother lives on the
farm. In the daytime they knock about on this road,
and they come home at dusk along with the cattle.
. . . It's a good farm."

We saw the other two: a boy and a girl, as the driver
said. They were dressed exactly alike, in shapeless
garments with petticoat-like skirts. The imperfect
thing that lived within them moved those beings to
howl at us from the top of the bank, where they sprawled
amongst the tough stalks of furze. Their cropped
black heads stuck out from the bright yellow wall of
countless small blossoms. The faces were purple with
the strain of yelling; the voices sounded blank and
cracked like a mechanical imitation of old people's
voices; and suddenly ceased when we turned into a
lane.

I saw them many times in my wandering about the
country. They lived on that road, drifting along its
length here and there, according to the inexplicable
impulses of their monstrous darkness. They were an
offence to the sunshine, a reproach to empty heaven,
a blight on the concentrated and purposeful vigour of
the wild landscape. In time the story of their parents
shaped itself before me out of the listless answers to my
questions, out of the indifferent words heard in wayside
inns or on the very road those idiots haunted. Some
of it was told by an emaciated and sceptical old fellow
with a tremendous whip, while we trudged together
over the sands by the side of a two-wheeled cart loaded
with dripping seaweed. Then at other times other
people confirmed and completed the story: till it stood
at last before me, a tale formidable and simple, as they
always are, those disclosures of obscure trials endured
by ignorant hearts.

When he returned from his military service Jean-Pierre Bacadou found the old people very much aged. He remarked with pain that the work of the farm was not satisfactorily done. The father had not the energy of old days. The hands did not feel over them the eye of the master. Jean-Pierre noted with sorrow that the heap of manure in the courtyard before the only entrance to the house was not so large as it should have been. The fences were out of repair, and the cattle suffered from neglect. At home the mother was practically bedridden, and the girls chattered loudly in the big kitchen, unrebuked, from morning to night. He said to himself: "We must change all this." He talked the matter over with his father one evening when the rays of the setting sun entering the yard between the outhouses ruled the heavy shadows with luminous streaks. Over the manure heap floated a mist, opal-tinted and odorous, and the marauding hens would stop in their scratching to examine with a sudden glance of their round eye the two men, both lean and tall, talking in hoarse tones. The old man, all twisted with rheumatism and bowed with years of work, the younger bony and straight, spoke without gestures in the indifferent manner of peasants, grave and slow. But before the sun had set the father had submitted to the sensible arguments of the son. "It is not for me that I am speaking," insisted Jean-Pierre. "It is for the land. It's a pity to see it badly used. I am not impatient for myself." The old fellow nodded over his stick. "I dare say; I dare say," he muttered. "You may be right. Do what you like. It's the mother that will be pleased."

The mother was pleased with her daughter-in-law. Jean-Pierre brought the two-wheeled spring-cart with a rush into the yard. The gray horse galloped clumsily, and the bride and bridegroom, sitting side by side, were jerked backwards and forwards by the up and down motion of the shafts, in a manner regular and brusque. On the road the distanced wedding guests straggled in pairs and groups. The men advanced with heavy steps, swinging their idle arms. They were clad in town clothes; jackets cut with clumsy smartness, hard black hats, immense boots, polished highly. Their women all in simple black, with white caps and shawls of faded tints folded triangularly on the back, strolled lightly by their side. In front the violin sang a strident tune, and the biniou snored and hummed, while the player capered solemnly, lifting high his heavy clogs. The sombre procession drifted in and out of the narrow lanes, through sunshine and through shade, between fields and hedgerows, scaring the little birds that darted away in troops right and left. In the yard of Bacadou's farm the dark ribbon wound itself up into a mass of men and women pushing at the door with cries and greetings. The wedding dinner was remembered for months. It was a splendid feast in the orchard. Farmers of considerable means and excellent repute were to be found sleeping in ditches, all along the road to Treguier, even as late as the afternoon of the next day. All the countryside participated in the happiness of Jean-Pierre. He remained sober, and, together with his quiet wife, kept out of the way, letting father and mother reap their due of honour and thanks. But the next day he took hold strongly, and the old folks felt a shadow—precursor of the grave—fall upon them finally. The world is to the young.

When the twins were born there was plenty of room in the house, for the mother of Jean-Pierre had gone away to dwell under a heavy stone in the cemetery of Ploumar. On that day, for the first time since his son's marriage, the elder Bacadou, neglected by the cackling lot of strange women who thronged the kitchen, left in the morning his seat under the mantel of the fireplace, and went into the empty cow-house, shaking his white locks dismally. Grandsons were all very well, but he wanted his soup at midday. When shown the babies, he stared at them with a fixed gaze, and muttered something like: "It's too much." Whether he meant too much happiness, or simply commented upon the number of his descendants, it is impossible to say. He looked offended—as far as his old wooden face could express anything; and for days afterwards could be seen, almost any time of the day, sitting at the gate, with his nose over his knees, a pipe between his gums, and gathered up into a kind of raging concentrated sulkiness. Once he spoke to his son, alluding to the newcomers with a groan: "They will quarrel over the land." "Don't bother about that, father," answered Jean-Pierre, stolidly, and passed, bent double, towing a recalcitrant cow over his shoulder.

He was happy, and so was Susan, his wife. It was not an ethereal joy welcoming new souls to struggle, perchance to victory. In fourteen years both boys would be a help; and, later on, Jean-Pierre pictured two big sons striding over the land from patch to patch, wringing tribute from the earth beloved and fruitful. Susan was happy too, for she did not want to be spoken of as the unfortunate woman, and now she had children no one could call her that. Both herself and her husband had seen something of the larger world—he during the time of his service; while she had spent a year or so in Paris with a Breton family; but had been too home-sick to remain longer away from the hilly and green country, set in a barren circle of rocks and sands, where she had been born. She thought that one of the boys ought perhaps to be a priest, but said nothing to her husband, who was a republican, and hated the "crows," as he called the ministers of religion. The christening was a splendid affair. All the commune came to it, for the Bacadous were rich and influential, and, now and then, did not mind the expense. The grandfather had a new coat.

Some months afterwards, one evening when the kitchen had been swept, and the door locked, Jean-Pierre, looking at the cot, asked his wife: "What's the matter with those children?" And, as if these words, spoken calmly, had been the portent of misfortune, she answered with a loud wail that must have been heard across the yard in the pig-sty; for the pigs (the Bacadous had the finest pigs in the country) stirred and grunted complainingly in the night. The husband went on grinding his bread and butter slowly, gazing at the wall, the soup-plate smoking under his chin. He had returned late from the market, where he had overheard (not for the first time) whispers behind his back. He revolved the words in his mind as he drove back. "Simple! Both of them. . . . Never any use! . . . Well! May be, may be. One must see. Would ask his wife." This was her answer. He felt like a blow on his chest, but said only: "Go, draw me some cider. I am thirsty!"

She went out moaning, an empty jug in her hand. Then he arose, took up the light, and moved slowly towards the cradle. They slept. He looked at them sideways, finished his mouthful there, went back heavily, and sat down before his plate. When his wife returned he never looked up, but swallowed a couple of spoonfuls noisily, and remarked, in a dull manner—

"When they sleep they are like other people's children."

She sat down suddenly on a stool near by, and shook with a silent tempest of sobs, unable to speak. He finished his meal, and remained idly thrown back in his chair, his eyes lost amongst the black rafters of the ceiling. Before him the tallow candle flared red and straight, sending up a slender thread of smoke. The light lay on the rough, sunburnt skin of his throat; the sunk cheeks were like patches of darkness, and his aspect was mournfully stolid, as if he had ruminated with difficulty endless ideas. Then he said, deliberately—

"We must see . . . consult people. Don't cry. . . . They won't all be like that . . . surely! We must sleep now."

After the third child, also a boy, was born, Jean-Pierre went about his work with tense hopefulness. His lips seemed more narrow, more tightly compressed than before; as if for fear of letting the earth he tilled hear the voice of hope that murmured within his breast. He watched the child, stepping up to the cot with a heavy clang of sabots on the stone floor, and glanced in, along his shoulder, with that indifference which is like a deformity of peasant humanity. Like the earth they master and serve, those men, slow of eye and speech, do not show the inner fire; so that, at last, it becomes a question with them as with the earth, what there is in the core: heat, violence, a force mysterious and terrible —or nothing but a clod, a mass fertile and inert, cold and unfeeling, ready to bear a crop of plants that sustain life or give death.

The mother watched with other eyes; listened with otherwise expectant ears. Under the high hanging shelves supporting great sides of bacon overhead, her body was busy by the great fireplace, attentive to the pot swinging on iron gallows, scrubbing the long table

where the field hands would sit down directly to their
evening meal. Her mind remained by the cradle, night
and day on the watch, to hope and suffer. That child,
like the other two, never smiled, never stretched its
hands to her, never spoke; never had a glance of recog-
nition for her in its big black eyes, which could only
stare fixedly at any glitter, but failed hopelessly to
follow the brilliance of a sun-ray slipping slowly along
the floor. When the men were at work she spent long
days between her three idiot children and the childish
grandfather, who sat grim, angular, and immovable,
with his feet near the warm ashes of the fire. The
feeble old fellow seemed to suspect that there was
something wrong with his grandsons. Only once,
moved either by affection or by the sense of proprieties,
he attempted to nurse the youngest. He took the boy
up from the floor, clicked his tongue at him, and essayed
a shaky gallop of his bony knees. Then he looked
closely with his misty eyes at the child's face and
deposited him down gently on the floor again. And he
sat, his lean shanks crossed, nodding at the steam
escaping from the cooking-pot with a gaze senile and
worried.

Then mute affliction dwelt in Bacadou's farmhouse,
sharing the breath and the bread of its inhabitants;
and the priest of the Ploumar parish had great cause for
congratulation. He called upon the rich landowner,
the Marquis de Chavanes, on purpose to deliver himself
with joyful unction of solemn platitudes about the inscrutable ways of Providence. In the vast dimness of
the curtained drawing-room, the little man, resembling a
black bolster, leaned towards a couch, his hat on his
knees, and gesticulated with a fat hand at the elon-
gated, gracefully-flowing lines of the clear Parisian
toilette from within which the half-amused, half-bored

marquise listened with gracious languor. He was exulting and humble, proud and awed. The impossible had come to pass. Jean-Pierre Bacadou, the enraged republican farmer, had been to mass last Sunday —had proposed to entertain the visiting priests at the next festival of Ploumar! It was a triumph for the Church and for the good cause. "I thought I would come at once to tell Monsieur le Marquis. I know how anxious he is for the welfare of our country," declared the priest, wiping his face. He was asked to stay to dinner.

The Chavanes returning that evening, after seeing their guest to the main gate of the park, discussed the matter while they strolled in the moonlight, trailing their long shadows up the straight avenue of chestnuts. The marquis, a royalist of course, had been mayor of the commune which includes Ploumar, the scattered hamlets of the coast, and the stony islands that fringe the yellow flatness of the sands. He had felt his position insecure, for there was a strong republican element in that part of the country; but now the conversion of Jean-Pierre made him safe. He was very pleased. "You have no idea how influential those people are," he explained to his wife. "Now, I am sure, the next communal election will go all right. I shall be re-elected." "Your ambition is perfectly insatiable, Charles," exclaimed the marquise, gaily. "But, ma chère amie," argued the husband, seriously, "it's most important that the right man should be mayor this year, because of the elections to the Chamber. If you think it amuses me . . ."

Jean-Pierre had surrendered to his wife's mother. Madame Levaille was a woman of business, known and respected within a radius of at least fifteen miles. Thick-set and stout, she was seen about the country,

on foot or in an acquaintance's cart, perpetually moving, in spite of her fifty-eight years, in steady pursuit
of business. She had houses in all the hamlets, she
worked quarries of granite, she freighted coasters with
stone—even traded with the Channel Islands. She
was broad-cheeked, wide-eyed, persuasive in speech:
carrying her point with the placid and invincible
obstinacy of an old woman who knows her own mind.
She very seldom slept for two nights together in the
same house; and the wayside inns were the best places
to inquire in as to her whereabouts. She had either
passed, or was expected to pass there at six; or somebody, coming in, had seen her in the morning, or expected to meet her that evening. After the inns that
command the roads, the churches were the buildings
she frequented most. Men of liberal opinions would
induce small children to run into sacred edifices to see
whether Madame Levaille was there, and to tell her
that so-and-so was in the road waiting to speak to her—
about potatoes, or flour, or stones, or houses; and she
would curtail her devotions, come out blinking and
crossing herself into the sunshine; ready to discuss
business matters in a calm, sensible way across a table
in the kitchen of the inn opposite. Latterly she had
stayed for a few days several times with her son-in-law,
arguing against sorrow and misfortune with composed
face and gentle tones. Jean-Pierre felt the convictions
imbibed in the regiment torn out of his breast—not by
arguments, but by facts. Striding over his fields he
thought it over. There were three of them. Three!
All alike! Why? Such things did not happen to
everybody—to nobody he ever heard of. One—
might pass. But three! All three. Forever useless, to be fed while he lived and . . . What
would become of the land when he died? This must be

seen to. He would sacrifice his convictions. One day he told his wife—

"See what your God will do for us. Pay for some masses."

Susan embraced her man. He stood unbending, then turned on his heels and went out. But afterwards, when a black *soutane* darkened his doorway, he did not object; even offered some cider himself to the priest. He listened to the talk meekly; went to mass between the two women; accomplished what the priest called "his religious duties" at Easter. That morning he felt like a man who had sold his soul. In the afternoon he fought ferociously with an old friend and neighbour who had remarked that the priests had the best of it and were now going to eat the priest-eater. He came home dishevelled and bleeding, and happening to catch sight of his children (they were kept generally out of the way), cursed and swore incoherently, banging the table. Susan wept. Madame Levaille sat serenely unmoved. She assured her daughter that "It will pass;" and taking up her thick umbrella, departed in haste to see after a schooner she was going to load with granite from her quarry.

A year or so afterwards the girl was born. A girl. Jean-Pierre heard of it in the fields, and was so upset by the news that he sat down on the boundary wall and remained there till the evening, instead of going home as he was urged to do. A girl! He felt half cheated. However, when he got home he was partly reconciled to his fate. One could marry her to a good fellow—not to a good for nothing, but to a fellow with some understanding and a good pair of arms. Besides, the next may be a boy, he thought. Of course they would be all right. His new credulity knew of no doubt. The ill luck was broken. He spoke cheerily to his wife. She was also hopeful. Three priests came to that christening, and Madame Levaille was godmother. The child turned out an idiot too.

Then on market days Jean-Pierre was seen bargaining bitterly, quarrelsome and greedy; then getting drunk with taciturn earnestness; then driving home in the dusk at a rate fit for a wedding, but with a face gloomy enough for a funeral. Sometimes he would insist on his wife coming with him; and they would drive in the early morning, shaking side by side on the narrow seat above the helpless pig, that, with tied legs, grunted a melancholy sigh at every rut. The morning drives were silent; but in the evening, coming home, Jean-Pierre, tipsy, was viciously muttering, and growled at the confounded woman who could not rear children that were like anybody else's. Susan, holding on against the erratic swayings of the cart, pretended not to hear. Once, as they were driving through Ploumar, some obscure and drunken impulse caused him to pull up sharply opposite the church. The moon swam amongst light white clouds. The tombstones gleamed pale under the fretted shadows of the trees in the churchyard. Even the village dogs slept. Only the nightingales, awake, spun out the thrill of their song above the silence of graves. Jean-Pierre said thickly to his wife—

"What do you think is there?"

He pointed his whip at the tower—in which the big dial of the clock appeared high in the moonlight like a pallid face without eyes—and getting out carefully, fell down at once by the wheel. He picked himself up and climbed one by one the few steps to the iron gate of the churchyard. He put his face to the bars and called out indistinctly—

"Hey there! Come out!"

"Jean! Return! Return!" entreated his wife in low tones.

He took no notice, and seemed to wait there. The song of nightingales beat on all sides against the high walls of the church, and flowed back between stone crosses and flat gray slabs, engraved with words of hope and sorrow.

"Hey! Come out!" shouted Jean-Pierre, loudly.

The nightingales ceased to sing.

"Nobody?" went on Jean-Pierre. "Nobody there. A swindle of the crows. That's what this is. Nobody anywhere. I despise it. Allez! Houp!"

He shook the gate with all his strength, and the iron bars rattled with a frightful clanging, like a chain dragged over stone steps. A dog near by barked hurriedly. Jean-Pierre staggered back, and after three successive dashes got into his cart. Susan sat very quiet and still. He said to her with drunken severity—

"See? Nobody. I've been made a fool! Malheur! Somebody will pay for it. The next one I see near the house I will lay my whip on . . . on the black spine . . . I will. I don't want him in there . . . he only helps the carrion crows to rob poor folk. I am a man. . . . We will see if I can't have children like anybody else . . . now you mind. . . . They won't be all . . . all . . . . we see. . . ."

She burst out through the fingers that hid her face—

"Don't say that, Jean; don't say that, my man!"

He struck her a swinging blow on the head with the back of his hand and knocked her into the bottom of the cart, where she crouched, thrown about lamentably by every jolt. He drove furiously, standing up, brandishing his whip, shaking the reins over the gray horse that galloped ponderously, making the heavy harness leap upon his broad quarters. The country rang clamorous in the night with the irritated barking of farm dogs, that followed the rattle of wheels all along the road. A couple of belated wayfarers had only just time to step into the ditch. At his own gate he caught the post and was shot out of the cart head first. The horse went on slowly to the door. At Susan's piercing cries the farm hands rushed out. She thought him dead, but he was only sleeping where he fell, and cursed his men, who hastened to him, for disturbing his slumbers.

Autumn came. The clouded sky descended low upon the black contours of the hills; and the dead leaves danced in spiral whirls under naked trees, till the wind, sighing profoundly, laid them to rest in the hollows of bare valleys. And from morning till night one could see all over the land black denuded boughs, the boughs gnarled and twisted, as if contorted with pain, swaying sadly between the wet clouds and the soaked earth. The clear and gentle streams of summer days rushed discoloured and raging at the stones that barred the way to the sea, with the fury of madness bent upon suicide. From horizon to horizon the great road to the sands lay between the hills in a dull glitter of empty curves, resembling an unnavigable river of mud.

Jean-Pierre went from field to field, moving blurred and tall in the drizzle, or striding on the crests of rises, lonely and high upon the gray curtain of drifting clouds, as if he had been pacing along the very edge of the universe. He looked at the black earth, at the earth mute and promising, at the mysterious earth doing its work of life in death-like stillness under the veiled sorrow of the sky. And it seemed to him that to a man worse than childless there was no promise in the fertility of fields, that from him the earth escaped, defied him, frowned at him like the clouds, sombre and hurried above his head. Having to face alone his own fields, he felt the inferiority of man who passes away before the clod that remains. Must he give up the hope of having by his side a son who would look at the turned-up sods with a master's eye? A man that would think as he thought, that would feel as he felt; a man who would be part of himself, and yet remain to trample masterfully on that earth when he was gone? He thought of some distant relations, and felt savage enough to curse them aloud. They! Never! He turned homewards, going straight at the roof of his dwelling, visible between the enlaced skeletons of trees. As he swung his legs over the stile a cawing flock of birds settled slowly on the field; dropped down behind his back, noiseless and fluttering, like flakes of soot.

That day Madame Levaille had gone early in the afternoon to the house she had near Kervanion. She had to pay some of the men who worked in her granite quarry there, and she went in good time because her little house contained a shop where the workmen could spend their wages without the trouble of going to town. The house stood alone amongst rocks. A lane of mud and stones ended at the door. The sea-winds coming ashore on Stonecutter's point, fresh from the fierce turmoil of the waves, howled violently at the unmoved heaps of black boulders holding up steadily short-armed, high crosses against the tremendous rush of the invisible. In the sweep of gales the sheltered dwelling stood in a calm resonant and disquieting, like the calm in the centre of a hurricane. On stormy nights, when the tide was out, the bay of Fougère, fifty feet below the house, resembled an immense black pit, from which ascended mutterings and sighs as if the sands down there had been alive and complaining. At high tide the returning water assaulted the ledges of rock in short rushes, ending in bursts of livid light and columns of spray, that flew inland, stinging to death the grass of pastures.

The darkness came from the hills, flowed over the coast, put out the red fires of sunset, and went on to seaward pursuing the retiring tide. The wind dropped with the sun, leaving a maddened sea and a devastated sky. The heavens above the house seemed to be draped in black rags, held up here and there by pins of fire. Madame Levaille, for this evening the servant of her own workmen, tried to induce them to depart. "An old woman like me ought to be in bed at this late hour," she good-humouredly repeated. The quarrymen drank, asked for more. They shouted over the table as if they had been talking across a field. At one end four of them played cards, banging the wood with their hard knuckles, and swearing at every lead. One sat with a lost gaze, humming a bar of some song, which he repeated endlessly. Two others, in a corner, were quarrelling confidentially and fiercely over some woman, looking close into one another's eyes as if they had wanted to tear them out, but speaking in whispers that promised violence and murder discreetly, in a venomous sibillation of subdued words. The atmosphere in there was thick enough to slice with a knife. Three candles burning about the long room glowed red and dull like sparks expiring in ashes.

The slight click of the iron latch was at that late hour as unexpected and startling as a thunder-clap. Madame Levaille put down a bottle she held above a liqueur glass; the players turned their heads; the whispered quarrel ceased; only the singer, after darting a glance at the door, went on humming with a stolid face. Susan appeared in the doorway, stepped in, flung the door to, and put her back against it, saying, half aloud—

"Mother!"

Madame Levaille, taking up the bottle again, said calmly: "Here you are, my girl. What a state you are in!" The neck of the bottle rang on the rim of the glass, for the old woman was startled, and the idea that the farm had caught fire had entered her head. She could think of no other cause for her daughter's appearance.

Susan, soaked and muddy, stared the whole length of the room towards the men at the far end. Her mother asked—

"What has happened? God guard us from misfortune!"

Susan moved her lips. No sound came. Madame Levaille stepped up to her daughter, took her by the arm, looked into her face.

"In God's name," she said, shakily, "what's the matter? You have been rolling in mud. . . . Why did you come? . . . Where's Jean?"

The men had all got up and approached slowly, staring with dull surprise. Madame Levaille jerked her daughter away from the door, swung her round upon a seat close to the wall. Then she turned fiercely to the men—

"Enough of this! Out you go—you others! I close."

One of them observed, looking down at Susan collapsed on the seat: "She is—one may say—half dead."

Madame Levaille flung the door open.

"Get out! March!" she cried, shaking nervously.

They dropped out into the night, laughing stupidly.

Outside, the two Lotharios broke out into loud shouts. The others tried to soothe them, all talking at once. The noise went away up the lane with the men, who staggered together in a tight knot, remonstrating with one another foolishly.

"Speak, Susan. What is it? Speak!" entreated Madame Levaille, as soon as the door was shut.

Susan pronounced some incomprehensible words, glaring at the table. The old woman clapped her hands above her head, let them drop, and stood looking at her daughter with disconsolate eyes. Her husband had been "deranged in his head" for a few years before he died, and now she began to suspect her daughter was going mad. She asked, pressingly—

"Does Jean know where you are? Where is Jean?"

Susan pronounced with difficulty—

"He knows . . . he is dead."

"What!" cried the old woman. She came up near, and peering at her daughter, repeated three times: "What do you say? What do you say? What do you say?"

Susan sat dry-eyed and stony before Madame Levaille, who contemplated her, feeling a strange sense of inexplicable horror creep into the silence of the house. She had hardly realised the news, further than to understand that she had been brought in one short moment face to face with something unexpected and final. It did not even occur to her to ask for any explanation. She thought: accident—terrible accident—blood to the head—fell down a trap door in the loft. . . . She remained there, distracted and mute, blinking her old eyes.

Suddenly, Susan said—

"I have killed him."

For a moment the mother stood still, almost unbreathing, but with composed face. The next second she burst out into a shout—

"You miserable madwoman . . . they will cut your neck. . . ."

She fancied the gendarmes entering the house, saying to her: "We want your daughter; give her up:" the gendarmes with the severe, hard faces of men on duty. She knew the brigadier well—an old friend, familiar and respectful, saying heartily, "To your good health, Madame!" before lifting to his lips the small glass of cognac—out of the special bottle she kept for friends. And now! . . . She was losing her head. She rushed here and there, as if looking for something urgently needed—gave that up, stood stock still in the middle of the room, and screamed at her daughter—

"Why? Say! Say! Why?"

The other seemed to leap out of her strange apathy.

"Do you think I am made of stone?" she shouted back, striding towards her mother.

"No! It's impossible. . . ." said Madame Levaille, in a convinced tone.

"You go and see, mother," retorted Susan, looking at her with blazing eyes. "There's no mercy in heaven —no justice. No! . . . I did not know. . . . Do you think I have no heart? Do you think I have never heard people jeering at me, pitying me, wondering at me? Do you know how some of them were calling me? The mother of idiots—that was my nickname! And my children never would know me, never speak to me. They would know nothing; neither men—nor God. Haven't I prayed! But the Mother of God herself would not hear me. A mother! . . . Who is accursed—I, or the man who is dead? Eh? Tell me. I took care of myself. Do you think I would defy the anger of God and have my house full of

those things—that are worse than animals who know
the hand that feeds them? Who blasphemed in the
night at the very church door? Was it I? . . . I
only wept and prayed for mercy . . . and I feel
the curse at every moment of the day—I see it round me
from morning to night . . . I've got to keep them
alive—to take care of my misfortune and shame. And
he would come. I begged him and Heaven for mercy.
. . . No! . . . Then we shall see. . . . He
came this evening. I thought to myself: 'Ah! again!'
. . . I had my long scissors. I heard him shouting
. . . I saw him near. . . . I must—must I?
. . . Then take! . . . And I struck him in the
throat above the breastbone. . . . I never heard
him even sigh. . . . I left him standing. . . .
It was a minute ago. How did I come here?"

Madame Levaille shivered. A wave of cold ran down
her back, down her fat arms under her tight sleeves,
made her stamp gently where she stood. Quivers ran
over the broad cheeks, across the thin lips, ran amongst
the wrinkles at the corners of her steady old eyes. She
stammered—

"You wicked woman—you disgrace me. But there!
You always resembled your father. What do you
think will become of you . . . in the other world?
In this . . . Oh misery!"

She was very hot now. She felt burning inside.
She wrung her perspiring hands—and suddenly, starting in great haste, began to look for her big shawl and
umbrella, feverishly, never once glancing at her daughter, who stood in the middle of the room following her
with a gaze distracted and cold.

"Nothing worse than in this," said Susan.

Her mother, umbrella in hand and trailing the shawl
over the floor, groaned profoundly.

"I must go to the priest," she burst out passionately. "I do not know whether you even speak the truth! You are a horrible woman. They will find you anywhere. You may stay here—or go. There is no room for you in this world."

Ready now to depart, she yet wandered aimlessly about the room, putting the bottles on the shelf, trying to fit with trembling hands the covers on cardboard boxes. Whenever the real sense of what she had heard emerged for a second from the haze of her thoughts she would fancy that something had exploded in her brain without, unfortunately, bursting her head to pieces—which would have been a relief. She blew the candles out one by one without knowing it, and was horribly startled by the darkness. She fell on a bench and began to whimper. After a while she ceased, and sat listening to the breathing of her daughter, whom she could hardly see, still and upright, giving no other sign of life. She was becoming old rapidly at last, during those minutes. She spoke in tones unsteady, cut about by the rattle of teeth, like one shaken by a deadly cold fit of ague.

"I wish you had died little. I will never dare to show my old head in the sunshine again. There are worse misfortunes than idiot children. I wish you had been born to me simple—like your own. . . ."

She saw the figure of her daughter pass before the faint and livid clearness of a window. Then it appeared in the doorway for a second, and the door swung to with a clang. Madame Levaille, as if awakened by the noise from a long nightmare, rushed out.

"Susan!" she shouted from the doorstep.

She heard a stone roll a long time down the declivity of the rocky beach above the sands. She stepped forward cautiously, one hand on the wall of the house, and peered down into the smooth darkness of the empty bay. Once again she cried—

"Susan! You will kill yourself there."

The stone had taken its last leap in the dark, and she heard nothing now. A sudden thought seemed to strangle her, and she called no more. She turned her back upon the black silence of the pit and went up the lane towards Ploumar, stumbling along with sombre determination, as if she had started on a desperate journey that would last, perhaps, to the end of her life. A sullen and periodic clamour of waves rolling over reefs followed her far inland between the high hedges sheltering the gloomy solitude of the fields.

Susan had run out, swerving sharp to the left at the door, and on the edge of the slope crouched down behind a boulder. A dislodged stone went on downwards, rattling as it leaped. When Madame Levaille called out, Susan could have, by stretching her hand, touched her mother's skirt, had she had the courage to move a limb. She saw the old woman go away, and she remained still, closing her eyes and pressing her side to the hard and rugged surface of the rock. After a while a familiar face with fixed eyes and an open mouth became visible in the intense obscurity amongst the boulders. She uttered a low cry and stood up. The face vanished, leaving her to gasp and shiver alone in the wilderness of stone heaps. But as soon as she had crouched down again to rest, with her head against the rock, the face returned, came very near, appeared eager to finish the speech that had been cut short by death, only a moment ago. She scrambled quickly to her feet and said: "Go away, or I will do it again." The thing wavered, swung to the right, to the left. She moved this way and that, stepped back, fancied herself screaming at it, and was appalled by the unbroken stillness of the night.

She tottered on the brink, felt the steep declivity under her feet, and rushed down blindly to save herself from a headlong fall. The shingle seemed to wake up; the pebbles began to roll before her, pursued her from above, raced down with her on both sides, rolling past with an increasing clatter. In the peace of the night the noise grew, deepening to a rumour, continuous and violent, as if the whole semicircle of the stony beach had started to tumble down into the bay. Susan's feet hardly touched the slope that seemed to run down with her. At the bottom she stumbled, shot forward, throwing her arms out, and fell heavily. She jumped up at once and turned swiftly to look back, her clenched hands full of sand she had clutched in her fall. The face was there, keeping its distance, visible in its own sheen that made a pale stain in the night. She shouted, "Go away!"—she shouted at it with pain, with fear, with all the rage of that useless stab that could not keep him quiet, keep him out of her sight. What did he want now? He was dead. Dead men have no children. Would he never leave her alone? She shrieked at it—waved her outstretched hands. She seemed to feel the breath of parted lips, and, with a long cry of discouragement, fled across the level bottom of the bay.

She ran lightly, unaware of any effort of her body. High sharp rocks that, when the bay is full, show above the glittering plain of blue water like pointed towers of submerged churches, glided past her, rushing to the land at a tremendous pace. To the left, in the distance, she could see something shining: a broad disc of light in which narrow shadows pivoted round the centre like the spokes of a wheel. She heard a voice calling, "Hey! There!" and answered with a wild scream. So, he could call yet! He was calling after her to stop.

Never! . . . She tore through the night, past the startled group of seaweed-gatherers who stood round their lantern paralysed with fear at the unearthly screech coming from that fleeing shadow. The men leaned on their pitchforks staring fearfully. A woman fell on her knees, and, crossing herself, began to pray aloud. A little girl with her ragged skirt full of slimy seaweed began to sob despairingly, lugging her soaked burden close to the man who carried the light. Somebody said: "The thing ran out towards the sea." Another voice exclaimed: "And the sea is coming back! Look at the spreading puddles. Do you hear—you woman—there! Get up!" Several voices cried together. "Yes, let us be off! Let the accursed thing go to the sea!" They moved on, keeping close round the light. Suddenly a man swore loudly. He would go and see what was the matter. It had been a woman's voice. He would go. There were shrill protests from women—but his high form detached itself from the group and went off running. They sent an unanimous call of scared voices after him. A word, insulting and mocking, came back, thrown at them through darkness. A woman moaned. An old man said gravely: "Such things ought to be left alone." They went on slower, shuffling in the yielding sand and whispering to one another that Millot feared nothing, having no religion, but that it would end badly some day.

Susan met the incoming tide by the Raven islet and stopped, panting, with her feet in the water. She heard the murmur and felt the cold caress of the sea, and, calmer now, could see the sombre and confused mass of the Raven on one side and on the other the long white streak of Molène sands that are left high above the dry bottom of Fougère Bay at every ebb. She turned round and saw far away, along the starred background of the sky, the ragged outline of the coast. Above it, nearly facing her, appeared the tower of Ploumar Church; a slender and tall pyramid shooting up dark and pointed into the clustered glitter of the stars. She felt strangely calm. She knew where she was, and began to remember how she came there—and why. She peered into the smooth obscurity near her. She was alone. There was nothing there; nothing near her, either living or dead.

The tide was creeping in quietly, putting out long impatient arms of strange rivulets that ran towards the land between ridges of sand. Under the night the pools grew bigger with mysterious rapidity, while the great sea, yet far off, thundered in a regular rhythm along the indistinct line of the horizon. Susan splashed her way back for a few yards without being able to get clear of the water that murmured tenderly all around and, suddenly, with a spiteful gurgle, nearly took her off her feet. Her heart thumped with fear. This place was too big and too empty to die in. To-morrow they would do with her what they liked. But before she died she must tell them—tell the gentlemen in black clothes that there are things no woman can bear. She must explain how it happened. . . . She splashed through a pool, getting wet to the waist, too preoccupied to care. . . . She must explain. "He came in the same way as ever and said, just so: 'Do you think I am going to leave the land to those people from Morbihan that I do not know? Do you? We shall see! Come along, you creature of mischance!' And he put his arms out. Then, Messieurs, I said: 'Before God—never!' And he said, striding at me with open palms: 'There is no God to hold me! Do you understand, you useless carcase. I will do what I like.' And he took me by the shoulders. Then I, Messieurs, called to God for help, and next minute, while he was shaking me, I felt my long scissors in my hand. His shirt was unbuttoned, and, by the candle-light, I saw the hollow of his throat. I cried: 'Let go!' He was crushing my shoulders. He was strong, my man was! Then I thought: No! . . . Must I? . . . Then take!—and I struck in the hollow place. I never saw him fall. Never! Never! . . . Never saw him fall. . . . The old father never turned his head. He is deaf and childish, gentlemen. . . . Nobody saw him fall. I ran out . . . Nobody saw. . . ."

She had been scrambling amongst the boulders of the Raven and now found herself, all out of breath, standing amongst the heavy shadows of the rocky islet. The Raven is connected with the main land by a natural pier of immense and slippery stones. She intended to return home that way. Was he still standing there? At home. Home! Four idiots and a corpse. She must go back and explain. Anybody would understand. . . .

Below her the night or the sea seemed to pronounce distinctly—

"Aha! I see you at last!"

She started, slipped, fell; and without attempting to rise, listened, terrified. She heard heavy breathing, a clatter of wooden clogs. It stopped.

"Where the devil did you pass?" said an invisible man, hoarsely.

She held her breath. She recognized the voice. She had not seen him fall. Was he pursuing her there dead, or perhaps . . . alive?

She lost her head. She cried from the crevice where she lay huddled, "Never, never!"

"Ah! You are still there. You led me a fine dance. Wait, my beauty, I must see how you look after all this. You wait. . . ."

Millot was stumbling, laughing, swearing meaninglessly out of pure satisfaction, pleased with himself for having run down that fly-by-night. "As if there were such things as ghosts! Bah! It took an old African soldier to show those clodhoppers. . . . But it was curious. Who the devil was she?"

Susan listened, crouching. He was coming for her, this dead man. There was no escape. What a noise he made amongst the stones. . . . She saw his head rise up, then the shoulders. He was tall—her own man! His long arms waved about, and it was his own voice sounding a little strange . . . because of the scissors. She scrambled out quickly, rushed to the edge of the causeway, and turned round. The man stood still on a high stone, detaching himself in dead black on the glitter of the sky.

"Where are you going to?" he called, roughly.

She answered, "Home!" and watched him intensely. He made a striding, clumsy leap on to another boulder, and stopped again, balancing himself, then said—

"Ha! ha! Well, I am going with you. It's the least I can do. Ha! ha! ha!"

She stared at him till her eyes seemed to become glowing coals that burned deep into her brain, and yet she was in mortal fear of making out the well-known features. Below her the sea lapped softly against the rock with a splash continuous and gentle.

The man said, advancing another step—

"I am coming for you. What do you think?"

She trembled. Coming for her! There was no escape, no peace, no hope. She looked round despairingly. Suddenly the whole shadowy coast, the blurred

islets, the heaven itself, swayed about twice, then came
to a rest. She closed her eyes and shouted—

"Can't you wait till I am dead!"

She was shaken by a furious hate for that shade that
pursued her in this world, unappeased even by death
in its longing for an heir that would be like other
people's children.

"Hey! What?" said Millot, keeping his distance
prudently. He was saying to himself: "Look out!
Some lunatic. An accident happens soon."

She went on, wildly—

"I want to live. To live alone—for a week—for a
day. I must explain to them. . . . I would tear
you to pieces, I would kill you twenty times over rather
than let you touch me while I live. How many times
must I kill you—you blasphemer! Satan sends you
here. I am damned too!"

"Come," said Millot, alarmed and conciliating. "I
am perfectly alive! . . . Oh, my God!"

She had screamed, "Alive!" and at once vanished
before his eyes, as if the islet itself had swerved aside
from under her feet. Millot rushed forward, and fell
flat with his chin over the edge. Far below he saw the
water whitened by her struggles, and heard one shrill
cry for help that seemed to dart upwards along the
perpendicular face of the rock, and soar past, straight
into the high and impassive heaven.

Madame Levaille sat, dry-eyed, on the short grass
of the hill side, with her thick legs stretched out, and
her old feet turned up in their black cloth shoes. Her
clogs stood near by, and further off the umbrella lay
on the withered sward like a weapon dropped from
the grasp of a vanquished warrior. The Marquis of
Chavanes, on horseback, one gloved hand on thigh,

looked down at her as she got up laboriously, with
groans. On the narrow track of the seaweed-carts
four men were carrying inland Susan's body on a hand-
barrow, while several others straggled listlessly behind.
Madame Levaille looked after the procession. "Yes,
Monsieur le Marquis," she said dispassionately, in her
usual calm tone of a reasonable old woman. "There
are unfortunate people on this earth. I had only one
child. Only one! And they won't bury her in con-
secrated ground!"

Her eyes filled suddenly, and a short shower of tears
rolled down the broad cheeks. She pulled the shawl
close about her. The Marquis leaned slightly over in
his saddle, and said—

"It is very sad. You have all my sympathy. I
shall speak to the Curé. She was unquestionably
insane, and the fall was accidental. Millot says so
distinctly. Good-day, Madame."

And he trotted off, thinking to himself: "I must get
this old woman appointed guardian of those idiots,
and administrator of the farm. It would be much
better than having here one of those other Bacadous,
probably a red republican, corrupting my commune."

AN OUTPOST OF PROGRESS

I

THERE were two white men in charge of the trading station. Kayerts, the chief, was short and fat; Carlier, the assistant, was tall, with a large head and a very broad trunk perched upon a long pair of thin legs. The third man on the staff was a Sierra Leone nigger, who maintained that his name was Henry Price. However, for some reason or other, the natives down the river had given him the name of Makola, and it stuck to him through all his wanderings about the country. He spoke English and French with a warbling accent, wrote a beautiful hand, understood bookkeeping, and cherished in his innermost heart the worship of evil spirits. His wife was a negress from Loanda, very large and very noisy. Three children rolled about in sunshine before the door of his low, shed-like dwelling. Makola, taciturn and impenetrable, despised the two white men. He had charge of a small clay storehouse with a dried-grass roof, and pretended to keep a correct account of beads, cotton cloth, red kerchiefs, brass wire, and other trade goods it contained. Besides the storehouse and Makola's hut, there was only one large building in the cleared ground of the station. It was built neatly of reeds, with a verandah on all the four sides. There were three rooms in it. The one in the middle was the living-room, and had two rough tables and a few stools in it. The other two were the bedrooms for the white men. Each had a bedstead and a mosquito net for all furniture. The plank floor was littered with the belongings of the white men; open half-empty boxes, torn wearing apparel, old boots; all the things dirty, and all the things broken, that accumulate mysteriously round untidy men. There was also another dwelling-place some distance away from the buildings. In it, under a tall cross much out of the perpendicular, slept the man who had seen the beginning of all this; who had planned and had watched the construction of this outpost of progress. He had been, at home, an unsuccessful painter who, weary of pursuing fame on an empty stomach, had gone out there through high protections. He had been the first chief of that station. Makola had watched the energetic artist die of fever in the just finished house with his usual kind of "I told you so" indifference. Then, for a time, he dwelt alone with his family, his account books, and the Evil Spirit that rules the lands under the equator. He got on very well with his god. Perhaps he had propitiated him by a promise of more white men to play with, by and by. At any rate the director of the Great Trading Company, coming up in a steamer that resembled an enormous sardine box with a flat-roofed shed erected on it, found the station in good order, and Makola as usual quietly diligent. The director had the cross put up over the first agent's grave, and appointed Kayerts to the post. Carlier was told off as second in charge. The director was a man ruthless and efficient, who at times, but very imperceptibly, indulged in grim humour. He made a speech to Kayerts and Carlier, pointing out to them the promising aspect of their station. The nearest trading-post was about three hundred miles away. It was an exceptional opportunity for them to distinguish themselves and to earn percentages on the trade. This appointment was a favour done to beginners. Kayerts was moved almost to tears by his director's kindness. He would, he said, by doing his best, try to justify the flattering confidence, &c., &c. Kayerts had been in the Administration of the Telegraphs, and knew how to express himself correctly. Carlier, an ex-non-commissioned officer of cavalry in an army guaranteed from harm by several European Powers, was less impressed. If there were commissions to get, so much the better; and, trailing a sulky glance over the river, the forests, the impenetrable bush that seemed to cut off the station from the rest of the world, he muttered between his teeth, "We shall see, very soon."

Next day, some bales of cotton goods and a few cases of provisions having been thrown on shore, the sardine-box steamer went off, not to return for another six months. On the deck the director touched his cap to the two agents, who stood on the bank waving their hats, and turning to an old servant of the Company on his passage to headquarters, said, "Look at those two imbeciles. They must be mad at home to send me such specimens. I told those fellows to plant a vegetable garden, build new storehouses and fences, and construct a landing-stage. I bet nothing will be done! They won't know how to begin. I always thought the station on this river useless, and they just fit the station!"

"They will form themselves there," said the old stager with a quiet smile.

"At any rate, I am rid of them for six months," retorted the director.

The two men watched the steamer round the bend, then, ascending arm in arm the slope of the bank, returned to the station. They had been in this vast and

dark country only a very short time, and as yet always
in the midst of other white men, under the eye and
guidance of their superiors. And now, dull as they
were to the subtle influences of surroundings, they felt
themselves very much alone, when suddenly left un-
assisted to face the wilderness; a wilderness rendered
more strange, more incomprehensible by the mysterious
glimpses of the vigorous life it contained. They were
two perfectly insignificant and incapable individuals,
whose existence is only rendered possible through the
high organization of civilized crowds. Few men realize
that their life, the very essence of their character, their
capabilities and their audacities, are only the expression
of their belief in the safety of their surroundings. The
courage, the composure, the confidence; the emotions
and principles; every great and every insignificant
thought belongs not to the individual but to the crowd:
to the crowd that believes blindly in the irresistible force
of its institutions and of its morals, in the power of its
police and of its opinion. But the contact with pure
unmitigated savagery, with primitive nature and primitive man, brings sudden and profound trouble into
the heart. To the sentiment of being alone of one's
kind, to the clear perception of the loneliness of one's
thoughts, of one's sensations—to the negation of the
habitual, which is safe, there is added the affirmation
of the unusual, which is dangerous; a suggestion of
things vague, uncontrollable, and repulsive, whose dis-
composing intrusion excites the imagination and tries
the civilized nerves of the foolish and the wise alike.

Kayerts and Carlier walked arm in arm, drawing
close to one another as children do in the dark; and
they had the same, not altogether unpleasant, sense of
danger which one half suspects to be imaginary. They
chatted persistently in familiar tones. "Our station

is prettily situated," said one. The other assented
with enthusiasm, enlarging volubly on the beauties
of the situation. Then they passed near the grave.
"Poor devil!" said Kayerts. "He died of fever, didn't
he?" muttered Carlier, stopping short. "Why," retorted Kayerts, with indignation, "I've been told that
the fellow exposed himself recklessly to the sun. The
climate here, everybody says, is not at all worse than
at home, as long as you keep out of the sun. Do you
hear that, Carlier? I am chief here, and my orders are
that you should not expose yourself to the sun!" He
assumed his superiority jocularly, but his meaning was
serious. The idea that he would, perhaps, have to
bury Carlier and remain alone, gave him an inward
shiver. He felt suddenly that this Carlier was more
precious to him here, in the centre of Africa, than a
brother could be anywhere else. Carlier, entering into
the spirit of the thing, made a military salute and
answered in a brisk tone, "Your orders shall be at-
tended to, chief!" Then he burst out laughing, slapped
Kayerts on the back and shouted, "We shall let life
run easily here! Just sit still and gather in the ivory
those savages will bring. This country has its good
points, after all!" They both laughed loudly while
Carlier thought: "That poor Kayerts; he is so fat and
unhealthy. It would be awful if I had to bury him
here. He is a man I respect." . . . Before they
reached the verandah of their house they called one
another "my dear fellow."

The first day they were very active, pottering about
with hammers and nails and red calico, to put up curtains, make their house habitable and pretty; resolved
to settle down comfortably to their new life. For
them an impossible task. To grapple effectually with
even purely material problems requires more serenity

of mind and more lofty courage than people generally imagine. No two beings could have been more unfitted for such a struggle. Society, not from any tenderness, but because of its strange needs, had taken care of those two men, forbidding them all independent thought, all initiative, all departure from routine; and forbidding it under pain of death. They could only live on condition of being machines. And now, released from the fostering care of men with pens behind the ears, or of men with gold lace on the sleeves, they were like those lifelong prisoners who, liberated after many years, do not know what use to make of their freedom. They did not know what use to make of their faculties, being both, through want of practice, incapable of independent thought.

At the end of two months Kayerts often would say, "If it was not for my Melie, you wouldn't catch me here." Melie was his daughter. He had thrown up his post in the Administration of the Telegraphs, though he had been for seventeen years perfectly happy there, to earn a dowry for his girl. His wife was dead, and the child was being brought up by his sisters. He regretted the streets, the pavements, the cafés, his friends of many years; all the things he used to see, day after day; all the thoughts suggested by familiar things—the thoughts effortless, monotonous, and soothing of a Government clerk; he regretted all the gossip, the small enmities, the mild venom, and the little jokes of Government offices. "If I had had a decent brother-in-law," Carlier would remark, "a fellow with a heart, I would not be here." He had left the army and had made himself so obnoxious to his family by his laziness and impudence, that an exasperated brother-in-law had made superhuman efforts to procure him an appointment in the Company as a second-class agent. Having

not a penny in the world he was compelled to accept
this means of livelihood as soon as it became quite clear
to him that there was nothing more to squeeze out of
his relations. He, like Kayerts, regretted his old life.
He regretted the clink of sabre and spurs on a fine afternoon, the barrack-room witticisms, the girls of garrison
towns; but, besides, he had also a sense of grievance.
He was evidently a much ill-used man. This made
him moody, at times. But the two men got on well together in the fellowship of their stupidity and laziness.
Together they did nothing, absolutely nothing, and enjoyed the sense of the idleness for which they were paid.
And in time they came to feel something resembling
affection for one another.

They lived like blind men in a large room, aware only
of what came in contact with them (and of that only
imperfectly), but unable to see the general aspect
of things. The river, the forest, all the great land
throbbing with life, were like a great emptiness. Even
the brilliant sunshine disclosed nothing intelligible.
Things appeared and disappeared before their eyes in
an unconnected and aimless kind of way. The river
seemed to come from nowhere and flow nowhither. It
flowed through a void. Out of that void, at times,
came canoes, and men with spears in their hands would
suddenly crowd the yard of the station. They were
naked, glossy black, ornamented with snowy shells and
glistening brass wire, perfect of limb. They made an
uncouth babbling noise when they spoke, moved in a
stately manner, and sent quick, wild glances out of
their startled, never-resting eyes. Those warriors
would squat in long rows, four or more deep, before the
verandah, while their chiefs bargained for hours with
Makola over an elephant tusk. Kayerts sat on his
chair and looked down on the proceedings, under-

standing nothing. He stared at them with his round blue eyes, called out to Carlier, "Here, look! look at that fellow there—and that other one, to the left. Did you ever see such a face? Oh, the funny brute!"

Carlier, smoking native tobacco in a short wooden pipe, would swagger up twirling his moustaches, and surveying the warriors with haughty indulgence, would say—

"Fine animals. Brought any bone? Yes? It's not any too soon. Look at the muscles of that fellow—third from the end. I wouldn't care to get a punch on the nose from him. Fine arms, but legs no good below the knee. Couldn't make cavalry men of them." And after glancing down complacently at his own shanks, he always concluded: "Pah! Don't they stink! You, Makola! Take that herd over to the fetish" (the storehouse was in every station called the fetish, perhaps because of the spirit of civilization it contained) "and give them up some of the rubbish you keep there. I'd rather see it full of bone than full of rags."

Kayerts approved.

"Yes, yes! Go and finish that palaver over there, Mr. Makola. I will come round when you are ready, to weigh the tusk. We must be careful." Then turning to his companion: "This is the tribe that lives down the river; they are rather aromatic. I remember, they had been once before here. D'ye hear that row? What a fellow has got to put up with in this dog of a country! My head is split."

Such profitable visits were rare. For days the two pioneers of trade and progress would look on their empty courtyard in the vibrating brilliance of vertical sunshine. Below the high bank, the silent river flowed on glittering and steady. On the sands in the middle of the stream, hippos and alligators sunned themselves side by side. And stretching away in all directions, surrounding the insignificant cleared spot of the trading post, immense forests, hiding fateful complications of fantastic life, lay in the eloquent silence of mute greatness. The two men understood nothing, cared for nothing but for the passage of days that separated them from the steamer's return. Their predecessor had left some torn books. They took up these wrecks of novels, and, as they had never read anything of the kind before, they were surprised and amused. Then during long days there were interminable and silly discussions about plots and personages. In the centre of Africa they made acquaintance of Richelieu and of d'Artagnan, of Hawk's Eye and of Father Goriot, and of many other people. All these imaginary personages became subjects for gossip as if they had been living friends. They discounted their virtues, suspected their motives, decried their successes; were scandalized at their duplicity or were doubtful about their courage. The accounts of crimes filled them with indignation, while tender or pathetic passages moved them deeply. Carlier cleared his throat and said in a soldierly voice, "What nonsense!" Kayerts, his round eyes suffused with tears, his fat cheeks quivering, rubbed his bald head, and declared, "This is a splendid book. I had no idea there were such clever fellows in the world." They also found some old copies of a home paper. That print discussed what it was pleased to call "Our Colonial Expansion" in high-flown language. It spoke much of the rights and duties of civilization, of the sacredness of the civilizing work, and extolled the merits of those who went about bringing light, and faith and commerce to the dark places of the earth. Carlier and Kayerts read, wondered, and began to think better of themselves. Carlier said one evening, waving his hand about, "In a hundred years, there will be perhaps a town here. Quays, and warehouses, and barracks, and—and—billiard-rooms. Civilization, my boy, and virtue—and all. And then, chaps will read that two good fellows, Kayerts and Carlier, were the first civilized men to live in this very spot!" Kayerts nodded, "Yes, it is a consolation to think of that." They seemed to forget their dead predecessor; but, early one day, Carlier went out and replanted the cross firmly. "It used to make me squint whenever I walked that way," he explained to Kayerts over the morning coffee. "It made me squint, leaning over so much. So I just planted it upright. And solid, I promise you! I suspended myself with both hands to the cross-piece. Not a move. Oh, I did that properly."

At times Gobila came to see them. Gobila was the chief of the neighbouring villages. He was a gray-headed savage, thin and black, with a white cloth round his loins and a mangy panther skin hanging over his back. He came up with long strides of his skeleton legs, swinging a staff as tall as himself, and, entering the common room of the station, would squat on his heels to the left of the door. There he sat, watching Kayerts, and now and then making a speech which the other did not understand. Kayerts, without interrupting his occupation, would from time to time say in a friendly manner: "How goes it, you old image?" and they would smile at one another. The two whites had a liking for that old and incomprehensible creature, and called him Father Gobila. Gobila's manner was paternal, and he seemed really to love all white men. They all appeared to him very young, indistinguishably alike (except for stature), and he knew that they were all brothers, and also immortal. The death of the artist, who was the first white man whom he knew intimately, did not disturb this belief, because he was firmly convinced that the white stranger had pretended to die and got himself buried for some mysterious purpose of his own, into which it was useless to inquire. Perhaps it was his way of going home to his own country? At any rate, these were his brothers, and he transferred his absurd affection to them. They returned it in a way. Carlier slapped him on the back, and recklessly struck off matches for his amusement. Kayerts was always ready to let him have a sniff at the ammonia bottle. In short, they behaved just like that other white creature that had hidden itself in a hole in the ground. Gobila considered them attentively. Perhaps they were the same being with the other—or one of them was. He couldn't decide—clear up that mystery; but he remained always very friendly. In consequence of that friendship the women of Gobila's village walked in single file through the reedy grass, bringing every morning to the station, fowls, and sweet potatoes, and palm wine, and sometimes a goat. The Company never provisions the stations fully, and the agents required those local supplies to live. They had them through the good-will of Gobila, and lived well. Now and then one of them had a bout of fever, and the other nursed him with gentle devotion. They did not think much of it. It left them weaker, and their appearance changed for the worse. Carlier was hollow-eyed and irritable. Kayerts showed a drawn, flabby face above the rotundity of his stomach, which gave him a weird aspect. But being constantly together, they did not notice the change that took place gradually in their appearance, and also in their dispositions.

Five months passed in that way.

Then, one morning, as Kayerts and Carlier, lounging in their chairs under the verandah, talked about the approaching visit of the steamer, a knot of armed men came out of the forest and advanced towards the station. They were strangers to that part of the country. They were tall, slight, draped classically from neck to heel in blue fringed cloths, and carried percussion muskets over their bare right shoulders. Makola showed signs of excitement, and ran out of the storehouse (where he spent all his days) to meet these visitors. They came into the courtyard and looked about them with steady, scornful glances. Their leader, a powerful and determined-looking negro with bloodshot eyes, stood in front of the verandah and made a long speech. He gesticulated much, and ceased very suddenly.

There was something in his intonation, in the sounds of the long sentences he used, that startled the two whites. It was like a reminiscence of something not exactly familiar, and yet resembling the speech of civilized men. It sounded like one of those impossible languages which sometimes we hear in our dreams.

"What lingo is that?" said the amazed Carlier. "In the first moment I fancied the fellow was going to speak French. Anyway, it is a different kind of gibberish to what we ever heard."

"Yes," replied Kayerts. "Hey, Makola, what does he say? Where do they come from? Who are they?"

But Makola, who seemed to be standing on hot bricks, answered hurriedly, "I don't know. They come from very far. Perhaps Mrs. Price will understand. They are perhaps bad men."

The leader, after waiting for a while, said something sharply to Makola, who shook his head. Then the man, after looking round, noticed Makola's hut and walked over there. The next moment Mrs. Makola was heard speaking with great volubility. The other strangers—they were six in all—strolled about with an air of ease, put their heads through the door of the store-room, congregated round the grave, pointed under-standingly at the cross, and generally made themselves at home.

"I don't like those chaps—and, I say, Kayerts, they must be from the coast; they've got firearms," observed the sagacious Carlier.

Kayerts also did not like those chaps. They both, for the first time, became aware that they lived in con-ditions where the unusual may be dangerous, and that there was no power on earth outside of themselves to stand between them and the unusual. They became uneasy, went in and loaded their revolvers. Kayerts said, "We must order Makola to tell them to go away before dark."

The strangers left in the afternoon, after eating a meal prepared for them by Mrs. Makola. The im-mense woman was excited, and talked much with the visitors. She rattled away shrilly, pointing here and there at the forests and at the river. Makola sat apart and watched. At times he got up and whispered to his wife. He accompanied the strangers across the ravine at the back of the station-ground, and returned slowly looking very thoughtful. When questioned by the white men he was very strange, seemed not to under-stand, seemed to have forgotten French—seemed to have forgotten how to speak altogether. Kayerts and Carlier agreed that the nigger had had too much palm wine.

There was some talk about keeping a watch in turn, but in the evening everything seemed so quiet and peaceful that they retired as usual. All night they were disturbed by a lot of drumming in the villages.

A deep, rapid roll near by would be followed by another far off—then all ceased. Soon short appeals would rattle out here and there, then all mingle together, increase, become vigorous and sustained, would spread out over the forest, roll through the night, unbroken and ceaseless, near and far, as if the whole land had been one immense drum booming out steadily an appeal to heaven. And through the deep and tremendous noise sudden yells that resembled snatches of songs from a madhouse darted shrill and high in discordant jets of sound which seemed to rush far above the earth and drive all peace from under the stars.

Carlier and Kayerts slept badly. They both thought they had heard shots fired during the night—but they could not agree as to the direction. In the morning Makola was gone somewhere. He returned about noon with one of yesterday's strangers, and eluded all Kayerts' attempts to close with him: had become deaf apparently. Kayerts wondered. Carlier, who had been fishing off the bank, came back and remarked while he showed his catch, "The niggers seem to be in a deuce of a stir; I wonder what's up. I saw about fifteen canoes cross the river during the two hours I was there fishing." Kayerts, worried, said, "Isn't this Makola very queer to-day?" Carlier advised, "Keep all our men together in case of some trouble."

THERE were ten station men who had been left by the
Director. Those fellows, having engaged themselves
to the Company for six months (without having any
idea of a month in particular and only a very faint
notion of time in general), had been serving the cause
of progress for upwards of two years. Belonging to a
tribe from a very distant part of the land of darkness
and sorrow, they did not run away, naturally supposing
that as wandering strangers they would be killed by the
inhabitants of the country; in which they were right.
They lived in straw huts on the slope of a ravine overgrown with reedy grass, just behind the station buildings. They were not happy, regretting the festive
incantations, the sorceries, the human sacrifices of their
own land; where they also had parents, brothers,
sisters, admired chiefs, respected magicians, loved
friends, and other ties supposed generally to be human.
Besides, the rice rations served out by the Company
did not agree with them, being a food unknown to their
land, and to which they could not get used. Con-
sequently they were unhealthy and miserable. Had
they been of any other tribe they would have made up
their minds to die—for nothing is easier to certain
savages than suicide—and so have escaped from the
puzzling difficulties of existence. But belonging, as
they did, to a warlike tribe with filed teeth, they had
more grit, and went on stupidly living through disease
and sorrow. They did very little work, and had lost

their splendid physique. Carlier and Kayerts doctored them assiduously without being able to bring them back into condition again. They were mustered every morning and told off to different tasks—grass-cutting, fence-building, tree-felling, &c., &c., which no power on earth could induce them to execute efficiently. The two whites had practically very little control over them.

In the afternoon Makola came over to the big house and found Kayerts watching three heavy columns of smoke rising above the forests. "What is that?" asked Kayerts. "Some villages burn," answered Makola, who seemed to have regained his wits. Then he said abruptly: "We have got very little ivory; bad six months' trading. Do you like get a little more ivory?"

"Yes," said Kayerts, eagerly. He thought of percentages which were low.

"Those men who came yesterday are traders from Loanda who have got more ivory than they can carry home. Shall I buy? I know their camp."

"Certainly," said Kayerts. "What are those traders?"

"Bad fellows," said Makola, indifferently. "They fight with people, and catch women and children. They are bad men, and got guns. There is a great disturbance in the country. Do you want ivory?"

"Yes," said Kayerts. Makola said nothing for a while. Then: "Those workmen of ours are no good at all," he muttered, looking round. "Station in very bad order, sir. Director will growl. Better get a fine lot of ivory, then he say nothing."

"I can't help it; the men won't work," said Kayerts. "When will you get that ivory?"

"Very soon," said Makola. "Perhaps to-night. You leave it to me, and keep indoors, sir. I think you had better give some palm wine to our men to make a dance this evening. Enjoy themselves. Work better to-morrow. There's plenty palm wine—gone a little sour."

Kayerts said "yes," and Makola, with his own hands carried big calabashes to the door of his hut. They stood there till the evening, and Mrs. Makola looked into every one. The men got them at sunset. When Kayerts and Carlier retired, a big bonfire was flaring before the men's huts. They could hear their shouts and drumming. Some men from Gobila's village had joined the station hands, and the entertainment was a great success.

In the middle of the night, Carlier waking suddenly, heard a man shout loudly; then a shot was fired. Only one. Carlier ran out and met Kayerts on the verandah. They were both startled. As they went across the yard to call Makola, they saw shadows moving in the night. One of them cried, "Don't shoot! It's me, Price." Then Makola appeared close to them. "Go back, go back, please," he urged, "you spoil all." "There are strange men about," said Carlier. "Never mind; I know," said Makola. Then he whispered, "All right. Bring ivory. Say nothing! I know my business." The two white men reluctantly went back to the house, but did not sleep. They heard footsteps, whispers, some groans. It seemed as if a lot of men came in, dumped heavy things on the ground, squabbled a long time, then went away. They lay on their hard beds and thought: "This Makola is invaluable." In the morning Carlier came out, very sleepy, and pulled at the cord of the big bell. The station hands mustered every morning to the sound of the bell. That morning nobody came. Kayerts turned out also, yawning, Across the yard they saw Makola come out of his hut, a tin basin of soapy water in his hand. Makola, a civilized nigger, was very neat in his person. He threw the soapsuds skilfully over a wretched little yellow cur he had, then turning his face to the agent's house, he shouted from the distance, "All the men gone last night!"

They heard him plainly, but in their surprise they both yelled out together: "What!" Then they stared at one another. "We are in a proper fix now," growled Carlier. "It's incredible!" muttered Kayerts. "I will go to the huts and see," said Carlier, striding off. Makola coming up found Kayerts standing alone.

"I can hardly believe it," said Kayerts, tearfully. "We took care of them as if they had been our children."

"They went with the coast people," said Makola after a moment of hesitation.

"What do I care with whom they went—the ungrateful brutes!" exclaimed the other. Then with sudden suspicion, and looking hard at Makola, he added: "What do you know about it?"

Makola moved his shoulders, looking down on the ground. "What do I know? I think only. Will you come and look at the ivory I've got there? It is a fine lot. You never saw such."

He moved towards the store. Kayerts followed him mechanically, thinking about the incredible desertion of the men. On the ground before the door of the fetish lay six splendid tusks.

"What did you give for it?" asked Kayerts, after surveying the lot with satisfaction.

"No regular trade," said Makola. "They brought the ivory and gave it to me. I told them to take what they most wanted in the station. It is a beautiful lot. No station can show such tusks. Those traders wanted carriers badly, and our men were no good here. No trade, no entry in books; all correct."

Kayerts nearly burst with indignation. "Why!" he shouted, "I believe you have sold our men for these tusks!" Makola stood impassive and silent. "I—I—will—I," stuttered Kayerts. "You fiend!" he yelled out.

"I did the best for you and the Company," said Makola, imperturbably. "Why you shout so much? Look at this tusk."

"I dismiss you! I will report you—I won't look at the tusk. I forbid you to touch them. I order you to throw them into the river. You—you!"

"You very red, Mr. Kayerts. If you are so irritable in the sun, you will get fever and die—like the first chief!" pronounced Makola impressively.

They stood still, contemplating one another with intense eyes, as if they had been looking with effort across immense distances. Kayerts shivered. Makola had meant no more than he said, but his words seemed to Kayerts full of ominous menace! He turned sharply and went away to the house. Makola retired into the bosom of his family; and the tusks, left lying before the store, looked very large and valuable in the sunshine.

Carlier came back on the verandah. "They're all gone, hey?" asked Kayerts from the far end of the common room in a muffled voice. "You did not find anybody?"

"Oh, yes," said Carlier, "I found one of Gobila's people lying dead before the huts—shot through the body. We heard that shot last night."

Kayerts came out quickly. He found his companion staring grimly over the yard at the tusks, away by the store. They both sat in silence for a while. Then Kayerts related his conversation with Makola. Carlier said nothing. At the midday meal they ate very little. They hardly exchanged a word that day. A great silence seemed to lie heavily over the station and press on their lips. Makola did not open the store; he spent the day playing with his children. He lay full-length on a mat outside his door, and the youngsters sat on his chest and clambered all over him. It was a touching picture. Mrs. Makola was busy cooking all day as usual. The white men made a somewhat better meal in the evening. Afterwards, Carlier smoking his pipe strolled over to the store; he stood for a long time over the tusks, touched one or two with his foot, even tried to lift the largest one by its small end. He came back to his chief, who had not stirred from the verandah, threw himself in the chair and said—

"I can see it! They were pounced upon while they slept heavily after drinking all that palm wine you've allowed Makola to give them. A put-up job! See? The worst is, some of Gobila's people were there, and got carried off too, no doubt. The least drunk woke up, and got shot for his sobriety. This is a funny country. What will you do now?"

"We can't touch it, of course," said Kayerts.

"Of course not," assented Carlier.

"Slavery is an awful thing," stammered out Kayerts in an unsteady voice.

"Frightful—the sufferings," grunted Carlier with conviction.

They believed their words. Everybody shows a respectful deference to certain sounds that he and his fellows can make. But about feelings people really know nothing. We talk with indignation or enthusiasm; we talk about oppression, cruelty, crime, devotion, self-sacrifice, virtue, and we know nothing real beyond the words. Nobody knows what suffering or sacrifice mean—except, perhaps the victims of the mysterious purpose of these illusions.

Next morning they saw Makola very busy setting up in the yard the big scales used for weighing ivory. By and by Carlier said: "What's that filthy scoundrel up to?" and lounged out into the yard. Kayerts followed. They stood watching. Makola took no notice. When the balance was swung true, he tried to lift a tusk into the scale. It was too heavy. He looked up helplessly without a word, and for a minute they stood round that balance as mute and still as three statues. Suddenly Carlier said: "Catch hold of the other end, Makola—you beast!" and together they swung the tusk up. Kayerts trembled in every limb. He muttered, "I say! O! I say!" and putting his hand in his pocket found there a dirty bit of paper and the stump of a pencil. He turned his back on the others, as if about to do something tricky, and noted stealthily the weights which Carlier shouted out to him with unnecessary loudness. When all was over Makola whispered to himself: "The sun's very strong here for the tusks." Carlier said to Kayerts in a careless tone: "I say, chief, I might just as well give him a lift with this lot into the store."

As they were going back to the house Kayerts observed with a sigh: "It had to be done." And Carlier said: "It's deplorable, but, the men being Company's men the ivory is Company's ivory. We must look after it." "I will report to the Director, of course," said Kayerts. "Of course; let him decide," approved Carlier.

At midday they made a hearty meal. Kayerts sighed from time to time. Whenever they mentioned Makola's name they always added to it an opprobrious epithet. It eased their conscience. Makola gave himself a half-holiday, and bathed his children in the river. No one from Gobila's villages came near the station that day. No one came the next day, and the next, nor for a whole week. Gobila's people might have been dead and buried for any sign of life they gave. But they were only mourning for those they had lost by the witchcraft of white men, who had brought wicked people into their country. The wicked people were gone, but fear remained. Fear always remains. A man may destroy everything within himself, love and hate and belief, and even doubt; but as long as he clings to life he cannot destroy fear: the fear, subtle, indestructible, and terrible, that pervades his being; that tinges his thoughts; that lurks in his heart; that watches on his lips the struggle of his last breath. In his fear, the mild old Gobila offered extra human sacrifices to all the Evil Spirits that had taken possession of his white friends. His heart was heavy. Some warriors spoke about burning and killing, but the cautious old savage dissuaded them. Who could foresee the woe those mysterious creatures, if irritated, might bring? They should be left alone. Perhaps in time they would disappear into the earth as the first one had disappeared. His people must keep away from them, and hope for the best.

Kayerts and Carlier did not disappear, but remained above on this earth, that, somehow, they fancied had become bigger and very empty. It was not the absolute and dumb solitude of the post that impressed them so much as an inarticulate feeling that something from within them was gone, something that worked for their safety, and had kept the wilderness from interfering with their hearts. The images of home; the memory of people like them, of men that thought and felt as they used to think and feel, receded into distances made

indistinct by the glare of unclouded sunshine. And
out of the great silence of the surrounding wilderness,
its very hopelessness and savagery seemed to approach
them nearer, to draw them gently, to look upon them,
to envelop them with a solicitude irresistible, familiar,
and disgusting.

Days lengthened into weeks, then into months.
Gobila's people drummed and yelled to every new
moon, as of yore, but kept away from the station.
Makola and Carlier tried once in a canoe to open
communications, but were received with a shower of
arrows, and had to fly back to the station for dear life.
That attempt set the country up and down the river
into an uproar that could be very distinctly heard for
days. The steamer was late. At first they spoke of
delay jauntily, then anxiously, then gloomily. The
matter was becoming serious. Stores were running
short. Carlier cast his lines off the bank, but the river
was low, and the fish kept out in the stream. They
dared not stroll far away from the station to shoot.
Moreover, there was no game in the impenetrable
forest. Once Carlier shot a hippo in the river. They
had no boat to secure it, and it sank. When it floated
up it drifted away, and Gobila's people secured the
carcase. It was the occasion for a national holiday,
but Carlier had a fit of rage over it and talked about
the necessity of exterminating all the niggers before
the country could be made habitable. Kayerts mooned
about silently; spent hours looking at the portrait of
his Melie. It represented a little girl with long bleached
tresses and a rather sour face. His legs were much
swollen, and he could hardly walk. Carlier, under-
mined by fever, could not swagger any more, but kept
tottering about, still with a devil-may-care air, as became a man who remembered his crack regiment. He

had become hoarse, sarcastic, and inclined to say unpleasant things. He called it "being frank with you." They had long ago reckoned their percentages on trade, including in them that last deal of "this infamous Makola." They had also concluded not to say anything about it. Kayerts hesitated at first—was afraid of the Director.

"He has seen worse things done on the quiet," maintained Carlier, with a hoarse laugh. "Trust him! He won't thank you if you blab. He is no better than you or me. Who will talk if we hold our tongues? There is nobody here."

That was the root of the trouble! There was nobody there; and being left there alone with their weakness, they became daily more like a pair of accomplices than like a couple of devoted friends. They had heard nothing from home for eight months. Every evening they said, "To-morrow we shall see the steamer." But one of the Company's steamers had been wrecked, and the Director was busy with the other, relieving very distant and important stations on the main river. He thought that the useless station, and the useless men, could wait. Meantime Kayerts and Carlier lived on rice boiled without salt, and cursed the Company, all Africa, and the day they were born. One must have lived on such diet to discover what ghastly trouble the necessity of swallowing one's food may become. There was literally nothing else in the station but rice and coffee; they drank the coffee without sugar. The last fifteen lumps Kayerts had solemnly locked away in his box, together with a half-bottle of Cognâc, "in case of sickness," he explained. Carlier approved. "When one is sick," he said, "any little extra like that is cheering."

They waited. Rank grass began to sprout over the

courtyard. The bell never rang now. Days passed, silent, exasperating, and slow. When the two men spoke, they snarled; and their silences were bitter, as if tinged by the bitterness of their thoughts.

One day after a lunch of boiled rice, Carlier put down his cup untasted, and said: "Hang it all! Let's have a decent cup of coffee for once. Bring out that sugar, Kayerts!"

"For the sick," muttered Kayerts, without looking up.

"For the sick," mocked Carlier. "Bosh! . . . Well! I am sick."

"You are no more sick than I am, and I go without," said Kayerts in a peaceful tone.

"Come! out with that sugar, you stingy old slave-dealer."

Kayerts looked up quickly. Carlier was smiling with marked insolence. And suddenly it seemed to Kayerts that he had never seen that man before. Who was he? He knew nothing about him. What was he capable of? There was a surprising flash of violent emotion within him, as if in the presence of something undreamt-of, dangerous, and final. But he managed to pronounce with composure—

"That joke is in very bad taste. Don't repeat it."

"Joke!" said Carlier, hitching himself forward on his seat. "I am hungry—I am sick—I don't joke! I hate hypocrites. You are a hypocrite. You are a slave-dealer. I am a slave-dealer. There's nothing but slave-dealers in this cursed country. I mean to have sugar in my coffee to-day, anyhow!"

"I forbid you to speak to me in that way," said Kayerts with a fair show of resolution.

"You!—What?" shouted Carlier, jumping up.

Kayerts stood up also. "I am your chief," he began, trying to master the shakiness of his voice.

"What?" yelled the other. "Who's chief? There's no chief here. There's nothing here: there's nothing but you and I. Fetch the sugar—you pot-bellied ass."

"Hold your tongue. Go out of this room," screamed Kayerts. "I dismiss you—you scoundrel!"

Carlier swung a stool. All at once he looked dangerously in earnest. "You flabby, good-for-nothing civilian—take that!" he howled.

Kayerts dropped under the table, and the stool struck the grass inner wall of the room. Then, as Carlier was trying to upset the table, Kayerts in desperation made a blind rush, head low, like a cornered pig would do, and over-turning his friend, bolted along the verandah, and into his room. He locked the door, snatched his revolver, and stood panting. In less than a minute Carlier was kicking at the door furiously, howling, "If you don't bring out that sugar, I will shoot you at sight, like a dog. Now then—one —two—three. You won't? I will show you who's the master."

Kayerts thought the door would fall in, and scrambled through the square hole that served for a window in his room. There was then the whole breadth of the house between them. But the other was apparently not strong enough to break in the door, and Kayerts heard him running round. Then he also began to run laboriously on his swollen legs. He ran as quickly as he could, grasping the revolver, and unable yet to understand what was happening to him. He saw in succession Makola's house, the store, the river, the ravine, and the low bushes; and he saw all those things again as he ran for the second time round the house. Then again they flashed past him. That morning he could not have walked a yard without a groan.

And now he ran. He ran fast enough to keep out of sight of the other man.

Then as, weak and desperate, he thought, "Before I finish the next round I shall die," he heard the other man stumble heavily, then stop. He stopped also. He had the back and Carlier the front of the house, as before. He heard him drop into a chair cursing, and suddenly his own legs gave way, and he slid down into a sitting posture with his back to the wall. His mouth was as dry as a cinder, and his face was wet with perspiration—and tears. What was it all about? He thought it must be a horrible illusion; he thought he was dreaming; he thought he was going mad! After a while he collected his senses. What did they quarrel about? That sugar! How absurd! He would give it to him—didn't want it himself. And he began scrambling to his feet with a sudden feeling of security. But before he had fairly stood upright, a common-sense reflection occurred to him and drove him back into despair. He thought: "If I give way now to that brute of a soldier, he will begin this horror again to-morrow—and the day after—every day—raise other pretensions, trample on me, torture me, make me his slave—and I will be lost! Lost! The steamer may not come for days—may never come." He shook so that he had to sit down on the floor again. He shivered forlornly. He felt he could not, would not move any more. He was completely distracted by the sudden perception that the position was without issue—that death and life had in a moment become equally difficult and terrible.

All at once he heard the other push his chair back; and he leaped to his feet with extreme facility. He listened and got confused. Must run again! Right or left? He heard footsteps. He darted to the left.

grasping his revolver, and at the very same instant, as it seemed to him, they came into violent collision. Both shouted with surprise. A loud explosion took place between them; a roar of red fire, thick smoke; and Kayerts, deafened and blinded, rushed back thinking: "I am hit—it's all over." He expected the other to come round—to gloat over his agony. He caught hold of an upright of the roof—"All over!" Then he heard a crashing fall on the other side of the house, as if somebody had tumbled headlong over a chair—then silence. Nothing more happened. He did not die. Only his shoulder felt as if it had been badly wrenched, and he had lost his revolver. He was disarmed and helpless! He waited for his fate. The other man made no sound. It was a stratagem. He was stalking him now! Along what side? Perhaps he was taking aim this very minute!

After a few moments of an agony frightful and absurd, he decided to go and meet his doom. He was prepared for every surrender. He turned the corner, steadying himself with one hand on the wall; made a few paces, and nearly swooned. He had seen on the floor, protruding past the other corner, a pair of turned-up feet. A pair of white naked feet in red slippers. He felt deadly sick, and stood for a time in profound darkness. Then Makola appeared before him, saying quietly: "Come along, Mr. Kayerts. He is dead." He burst into tears of gratitude; a loud, sobbing fit of crying. After a time he found himself sitting in a chair and looking at Carlier, who lay stretched on his back. Makola was kneeling over the body.

"Is this your revolver?" asked Makola, getting up.

"Yes," said Kayerts; then he added very quickly, "He ran after me to shoot me—you saw!"

"Yes, I saw," said Makola. "There is only one revolver; where's his?"

"Don't know," whispered Kayerts in a voice that had become suddenly very faint.

"I will go and look for it," said the other, gently. He made the round along the verandah, while Kayerts sat still and looked at the corpse. Makola came back empty-handed, stood in deep thought, then stepped quietly into the dead man's room, and came out directly with a revolver, which he held up before Kayerts. Kayerts shut his eyes. Everything was going round. He found life more terrible and difficult than death. He had shot an unarmed man.

After meditating for a while, Makola said softly, pointing at the dead man who lay there with his right eye blown out—

"He died of fever." Kayerts looked at him with a stony stare. "Yes," repeated Makola, thoughtfully, stepping over the corpse, "I think he died of fever. Bury him to-morrow."

And he went away slowly to his expectant wife, leaving the two white men alone on the verandah.

Night came, and Kayerts sat unmoving on his chair. He sat quiet as if he had taken a dose of opium. The violence of the emotions he had passed through produced a feeling of exhausted serenity. He had plumbed in one short afternoon the depths of horror and despair, and now found repose in the conviction that life had no more secrets for him: neither had death! He sat by the corpse thinking; thinking very actively, thinking very new thoughts. He seemed to have broken loose from himself altogether. His old thoughts, convictions, likes and dislikes, things he respected and things he abhorred, appeared in their true light at last! Appeared contemptible and childish, false and ridiculous. He revelled in his new wisdom while he sat by the man he had killed. He argued with himself about all things

under heaven with that kind of wrong-headed lucidity
which may be observed in some lunatics. Incidentally
he reflected that the fellow dead there had been a
noxious beast anyway; that men died every day in
thousands; perhaps in hundreds of thousands—who
could tell?—and that in the number, that one death
could not possibly make any difference; couldn't have
any importance, at least to a thinking creature. He,
Kayerts, was a thinking creature. He had been all
his life, till that moment, a believer in a lot of nonsense
like the rest of mankind—who are fools; but now he
thought! He knew! He was at peace; he was familiar
with the highest wisdom! Then he tried to imagine
himself dead, and Carlier sitting in his chair watching
him; and his attempt met with such unexpected success,
that in a very few moments he became not at all sure
who was dead and who was alive. This extraordinary
achievement of his fancy startled him, however, and
by a clever and timely effort of mind he saved himself
just in time from becoming Carlier. His heart thumped,
and he felt hot all over at the thought of that danger.
Carlier! What a beastly thing! To compose his now
disturbed nerves—and no wonder!—he tried to whistle
a little. Then, suddenly, he fell asleep, or thought he
had slept; but at any rate there was a fog, and somebody had whistled in the fog.

He stood up. The day had come, and a heavy mist
had descended upon the land: the mist penetrating,
enveloping, and silent; the morning mist of tropical
lands; the mist that clings and kills; the mist white
and deadly, immaculate and poisonous. He stood up,
saw the body, and threw his arms above his head with
a cry like that of a man who, waking from a trance,
finds himself immured forever in a tomb. *"Help!
. . . . My God!"*

A shriek inhuman, vibrating and sudden, pierced like
a sharp dart the white shroud of that land of sorrow.
Three short, impatient screeches followed, and then,
for a time, the fog-wreaths rolled on, undisturbed,
through a formidable silence. Then many more shrieks,
rapid and piercing, like the yells of some exasperated
and ruthless creature, rent the air. Progress was calling to Kayerts from the river. Progress and civilization and all the virtues. Society was calling to its
accomplished child to come, to be taken care of, to be
instructed, to be judged, to be condemned; it called
him to return to that rubbish heap from which he had
wandered away, so that justice could be done.

Kayerts heard and understood. He stumbled out
of the verandah, leaving the other man quite alone
for the first time since they had been thrown there
together. He groped his way through the fog, calling
in his ignorance upon the invisible heaven to undo its
work. Makola flitted by in the mist, shouting as he
ran—

"Steamer! Steamer! They can't see. They whistle
for the station. I go ring the bell. Go down to the
landing, sir. I ring."

He disappeared. Kayerts stood still. He looked
upwards; the fog rolled low over his head. He looked
round like a man who has lost his way; and he saw a
dark smudge, a cross-shaped stain, upon the shifting
purity of the mist. As he began to stumble towards it,
the station bell rang in a tumultuous peal its answer to
the impatient clamour of the steamer.

The Managing Director of the Great Civilizing
Company (since we know that civilization follows
trade) landed first, and incontinently lost sight of the
steamer. The fog down by the river was exceedingly

dense; above, at the station, the bell rang unceasing and brazen.

The Director shouted loudly to the steamer:

"There is nobody down to meet us; there may be something wrong, though they are ringing. You had better come, too!"

And he began to toil up the steep bank. The captain and the engine-driver of the boat followed behind. As they scrambled up the fog thinned, and they could see their Director a good way ahead. Suddenly they saw him start forward, calling to them over his shoulder:
—"Run! Run to the house! I've found one of them. Run, look for the other!"

He had found one of them! And even he, the man of varied and startling experience, was somewhat discomposed by the manner of this finding. He stood and fumbled in his pockets (for a knife) while he faced Kayerts, who was hanging by a leather strap from the cross. He had evidently climbed the grave, which was high and narrow, and after tying the end of the strap to the arm, had swung himself off. His toes were only a couple of inches above the ground; his arms hung stiffly down; he seemed to be standing rigidly at attention, but with one purple cheek playfully posed on the shoulder. And, irreverently, he was putting out a swollen tongue at his Managing Director.

THE RETURN

The inner circle train from the City rushed impetuously out of a black hole and pulled up with a discordant, grinding racket in the smirched twilight of a West-End station. A line of doors flew open and a lot of men stepped out headlong. They had high hats, healthy pale faces, dark overcoats and shiny boots; they held in their gloved hands thin umbrellas and hastily folded evening papers that resembled stiff, dirty rags of greenish, pinkish, or whitish colour. Alvan Hervey stepped out with the rest, a smouldering cigar between his teeth. A disregarded little woman in rusty black, with both arms full of parcels, ran along in distress, bolted suddenly into a third-class compartment and the train went on. The slamming of carriage doors burst out sharp and spiteful like a fusillade; an icy draught mingled with acrid fumes swept the whole length of the platform and made a tottering old man, wrapped up to his ears in a woollen comforter, stop short in the moving throng to cough violently over his stick. No one spared him a glance.

Alvan Hervey passed through the ticket gate. Between the bare walls of a sordid staircase men clambered rapidly; their backs appeared alike—almost as if they had been wearing a uniform; their indifferent faces were varied but somehow suggested kinship, like the faces of a band of brothers who through prudence, dignity, disgust, or foresight would resolutely ignore each other; and their eyes, quick or slow; their eyes gazing up the dusty steps; their eyes brown, black, gray, blue, had all the same stare, concentrated and empty, satisfied and unthinking.

Outside the big doorway of the street they scattered in all directions, walking away fast from one another with the hurried air of men fleeing from something compromising; from familiarity or confidences; from something suspected and concealed—like truth or pestilence. Alvan Hervey hesitated, standing alone in the doorway for a moment; then decided to walk home.

He strode firmly. A misty rain settled like silvery dust on clothes, on moustaches; wetted the faces, varnished the flagstones, darkened the walls, dripped from umbrellas. And he moved on in the rain with careless serenity, with the tranquil ease of someone successful and disdainful, very sure of himself—a man with lots of money and friends. He was tall, well set-up, good-looking and healthy; and his clear pale face had under its commonplace refinement that slight tinge of overbearing brutality which is given by the possession of only partly difficult accomplishments; by excelling in games, or in the art of making money; by the easy mastery over animals and over needy men.

He was going home much earlier than usual, straight from the City and without calling at his club. He considered himself well connected, well educated and intelligent. Who doesn't? But his connections, education and intelligence were strictly on a par with those of the men with whom he did business or amused himself. He had married five years ago. At the time all his acquaintances had said he was very much in love; and he had said so himself, frankly, because it is very well understood that every man falls in love once in his life—unless his wife dies, when it may be quite praiseworthy to fall in love again. The girl was healthy, tall, fair, and in his opinion was well con-

nected, well educated and intelligent. She was also
intensely bored with her home where, as if packed in a
tight box, her individuality—of which she was very
conscious—had no play. She strode like a grenadier,
was strong and upright like an obelisk, had a beautiful
face, a candid brow, pure eyes, and not a thought of
her own in her head. He surrendered quickly to all
those charms, and she appeared to him so unquestionably of the right sort that he did not hesitate for a
moment to declare himself in love. Under the cover
of that sacred and poetical fiction he desired her
masterfully, for various reasons; but principally for
the satisfaction of having his own way. He was very
dull and solemn about it—for no earthly reason, unless
to conceal his feelings—which is an eminently proper
thing to do. Nobody, however, would have been
shocked had he neglected that duty, for the feeling he
experienced really was a longing—a longing stronger
and a little more complex no doubt, but no more
reprehensible in its nature than a hungry man's ap-
petite for his dinner.

After their marriage they busied themselves, with
marked success, in enlarging the circle of their acquaintance. Thirty people knew them by sight;
twenty more with smiling demonstrations tolerated
their occasional presence within hospitable thresholds;
at least fifty others became aware of their existence.
They moved in their enlarged world amongst perfectly
delightful men and women who feared emotion, enthusiasm, or failure, more than fire, war, or mortal
disease; who tolerated only the commonest formulas
of commonest thoughts, and recognized only profitable
facts. It was an extremely charming sphere, the abode
of all the virtues, where nothing is realized and where
all joys and sorrows are cautiously toned down into

pleasures and annoyances. In that serene region
then, where noble sentiments are cultivated in suffi-
cient profusion to conceal the pitiless materialism of
thoughts and aspirations Alvan Hervey and his wife
spent five years of prudent bliss unclouded by any
doubt as to the moral propriety of their existence.
She, to give her individuality fair play, took up all
manner of philanthropic work and became a member of
various rescuing and reforming societies patronized or
presided over by ladies of title. He took an active interest in politics; and having met quite by chance a literary
man—who nevertheless was related to an earl—he was
induced to finance a moribund society paper. It was a
semi-political, and wholly scandalous publication, re-
deemed by excessive dulness; and as it was utterly faithless, as it contained no new thought, as it never by any
chance had a flash of wit, satire, or indignation in its
pages, he judged it respectable enough, at first sight.
Afterwards, when it paid, he promptly perceived that
upon the whole it was a virtuous undertaking. It
paved the way of his ambition; and he enjoyed also
the special kind of importance he derived from this
connection with what he imagined to be literature.

This connection still further enlarged their world.
Men who wrote or drew prettily for the public came
at times to their house, and his editor came very often.
He thought him rather an ass because he had such big
front teeth (the proper thing is to have small, even
teeth) and wore his hair a trifle longer than most men
do. However, some dukes wear their hair long, and
the fellow indubitably knew his business. The worst
was that his gravity, though perfectly portentous,
could not be trusted. He sat, elegant and bulky, in
the drawing-room, the head of his stick hovering in
front of his big teeth, and talked for hours with a thick-

lipped smile (he said nothing that could be considered objectionable and not quite the thing) talked in an unusual manner—not obviously—irritatingly. His forehead was too lofty—unusually so—and under it there was a straight nose, lost between the hairless cheeks, that in a smooth curve ran into a chin shaped like the end of a snow-shoe. And in this face that resembled the face of a fat and fiendishly knowing baby there glittered a pair of clever, peering, unbelieving black eyes. He wrote verses too. Rather an ass. But the band of men who trailed at the skirts of his monumental frock-coat seemed to perceive wonderful things in what he said. Alvan Hervey put it down to affectation. Those artist chaps, upon the whole, were so affected. Still, all this was highly proper—very useful to him—and his wife seemed to like it—as if she also had derived some distinct and secret advantage from this intellectual connection. She received her mixed and decorous guests with a kind of tall, ponderous grace, peculiarly her own and which awakened in the mind of intimidated strangers incongruous and improper reminiscences of an elephant, a giraffe, a gazelle; of a gothic tower—of an overgrown angel. Her Thursdays were becoming famous in their world; and their world grew steadily, annexing street after street. It included also Somebody's Gardens, a Crescent—a couple of Squares.

Thus Alvan Hervey and his wife for five prosperous years lived by the side of one another. In time they came to know each other sufficiently well for all the practical purposes of such an existence, but they were no more capable of real intimacy than two animals feeding at the same manger, under the same roof, in a luxurious stable. His longing was appeased and became a habit; and she had her desire—the desire to get away from under the paternal roof, to assert her individuality, to move in her own set (so much smarter than the parental one); to have a home of her own, and her own share of the world's respect, envy, and applause. They understood each other warily, tacitly, like a pair of cautious conspirators in a profitable plot; because they were both unable to look at a fact, a sentiment, a principle, or a belief otherwise than in the light of their own dignity, of their own glorification, of their own advantage. They skimmed over the surface of life hand in hand, in a pure and frosty atmosphere—like two skilful skaters cutting figures on thick ice for the admiration of the beholders, and disdainfully ignoring the hidden stream, the stream restless and dark; the stream of life, profound and unfrozen.

Alvan Hervey turned twice to the left, once to the right, walked along two sides of a square, in the middle of which groups of tame-looking trees stood in respectable captivity behind iron railings, and rang at his door. A parlourmaid opened. A fad of his wife's, this, to have only women servants. That girl, while she took his hat and overcoat, said something which made him look at his watch. It was five o'clock, and his wife not at home. There was nothing unusual in that. He said, "No; no tea," and went upstairs.

He ascended without footfalls. Brass rods glimmered all up the red carpet. On the first-floor landing a marble woman, decently covered from neck to instep with stone draperies, advanced a row of lifeless toes to the edge of the pedestal, and thrust out blindly a rigid white arm holding a cluster of lights. He had artistic tastes—at home. Heavy curtains caught back, half concealed dark corners. On the rich, stamped paper of the walls hung sketches, watercolours, engravings. His tastes were distinctly artistic

Old church towers peeped above green masses of foliage;
the hills were purple, the sands yellow, the seas sunny,
the skies blue. A young lady sprawled with dreamy
eyes in a moored boat, in company of a lunch basket, a
champagne bottle, and an enamoured man in a blazer.
Bare-legged boys flirted sweetly with ragged maidens,
slept on stone steps, gambolled with dogs. A patheti-
cally lean girl flattened against a blank wall, turned up
expiring eyes and tendered a flower for sale; while, near
by, the large photographs of some famous and mutilated bas-reliefs seemed to represent a massacre turned
into stone.

He looked, of course, at nothing, ascended another
flight of stairs and went straight into the dressing room.
A bronze dragon nailed by the tail to a bracket writhed
away from the wall in calm convolutions, and held,
between the conventional fury of its jaws, a crude gas
flame that resembled a butterfly. The room was
empty, of course; but, as he stepped in, it became filled
all at once with a stir of many people; because the
strips of glass on the doors of wardrobes and his wife's
large pier-glass reflected him from head to foot, and
multiplied his image into a crowd of gentlemanly and
slavish imitators, who were dressed exactly like himself;
had the same restrained and rare gestures; who moved
when he moved, stood still with him in an obsequious
immobility, and had just such appearances of life and
feeling as he thought it dignified and safe for any man
to manifest. And like real people who are slaves of
common thoughts, that are not even their own, they
affected a shadowy independence by the superficial
variety of their movements. They moved together
with him; but they either advanced to meet him, or
walked away from him; they appeared, disappeared;
they seemed to dodge behind walnut furniture, to be

seen again, far within the polished panes, stepping about
distinct and unreal in the convincing illusion of a room.
And like the men he respected they could be trusted
to do nothing individual, original, or startling—nothing
unforeseen and nothing improper.

He moved for a time aimlessly in that good company,
humming a popular but refined tune, and thinking
vaguely of a business letter from abroad, which had to
be answered on the morrow with cautious prevarication.
Then, as he walked towards a wardrobe, he saw appear-
ing at his back, in the high mirror, the corner of his
wife's dressing-table, and amongst the glitter of silver-
mounted objects on it, the square white patch of an
envelope. It was such an unusual thing to be seen
there that he spun round almost before he realized his
surprise; and all the sham men about him pivoted on
their heels; all appeared surprised; and all moved
rapidly towards envelopes on dressing-tables.

He recognized his wife's handwriting and saw that
the envelope was addressed to himself. He muttered,
"How very odd," and felt annoyed. Apart from any
odd action being essentially an indecent thing in itself,
the fact of his wife indulging in it made it doubly offensive. That she should write to him at all, when she
knew he would be home for dinner, was perfectly
ridiculous; but that she should leave it like this—in
evidence for chance discovery—struck him as so out-
rageous that, thinking of it, he experienced suddenly
a staggering sense of insecurity, an absurd and bizarre
flash of a notion that the house had moved a little under
his feet. He tore the envelope open, glanced at the
letter, and sat down in a chair near by.

He held the paper before his eyes and looked at half
a dozen lines scrawled on the page, while he was stunned
by a noise meaningless and violent, like the clash of

gongs or the beating of drums; a great aimless uproar that, in a manner, prevented him from hearing himself think and made his mind an absolute blank. This absurd and distracting tumult seemed to ooze out of the written words, to issue from between his very fingers that trembled, holding the paper. And suddenly he dropped the letter as though it had been something hot, or venomous, or filthy; and rushing to the window with the unreflecting precipitation of a man anxious to raise an alarm of fire or murder, he threw it up and put his head out.

A chill gust of wind, wandering through the damp and sooty obscurity over the waste of roofs and chimney-pots, touched his face with a clammy flick. He saw an illimitable darkness, in which stood a black jumble of walls, and, between them, the many rows of gaslights stretched far away in long lines, like strung-up beads of fire. A sinister loom as of a hidden conflagration lit up faintly from below the mist, falling upon a billowy and motionless sea of tiles and bricks. At the rattle of the opened window the world seemed to leap out of the night and confront him, while floating up to his ears there came a sound vast and faint; the deep mutter of something immense and alive. It penetrated him with a feeling of dismay and he gasped silently. From the cab-stand in the square came distinct hoarse voices and a jeering laugh which sounded ominously harsh and cruel. It sounded threatening. He drew his head in, as if before an aimed blow, and flung the window down quickly. He made a few steps, stumbled against a chair, and with a great effort, pulled himself together to lay hold of a certain thought that was whizzing about loose in his head.

He got it at last, after more exertion than he expected; he was flushed and puffed a little as though he had been catching it with his hands, but his mental hold on it was weak, so weak that he judged it necessary to repeat it aloud—to hear it spoken firmly—in order to insure a perfect measure of possession. But he was unwilling to hear his own voice—to hear any sound whatever— owing to a vague belief, shaping itself slowly within him, that solitude and silence are the greatest felicities of mankind. The next moment it dawned upon him that they are perfectly unattainable—that faces must be seen, words spoken, thoughts heard. All the words —all the thoughts!

He said very distinctly, and looking at the carpet, "She's gone."

It was terrible—not the fact but the words; the words charged with the shadowy might of a meaning, that seemed to possess the tremendous power to call Fate down upon the earth, like those strange and appalling words that sometimes are heard in sleep. They vibrated round him in a metallic atmosphere, in a space that had the hardness of iron and the resonance of a bell of bronze. Looking down between the toes of his boots he seemed to listen thoughtfully to the receding wave of sound; to the wave spreading out in a widening circle, embracing streets, roofs, church-steeples, fields—and travelling away, widening endlessly, far, very far, where he could not hear—where he could not imagine anything—where . . .

"And—with that . . . ass," he said again without stirring in the least. And there was nothing but humiliation. Nothing else. He could derive no moral solace from any aspect of the situation, which radiated pain only on every side. Pain. What kind of pain? It occurred to him that he ought to be heart-broken; but in an exceedingly short moment he perceived that his suffering was nothing of so trifling and dignified a kind. It was altogether a more serious matter, and partook rather of the nature of those subtle and cruel feelings which are awakened by a kick or a horse-whipping.

He felt very sick—physically sick—as though he had bitten through something nauseous. Life, that to a well-ordered mind should be a matter of congratulation, appeared to him, for a second or so, perfectly intolerable. He picked up the paper at his feet, and sat down with the wish to think it out, to understand why his wife—his wife!—should leave him, should throw away respect, comfort, peace, decency, position—throw away everything for nothing! He set himself to think out the hidden logic of her action—a mental undertaking fit for the leisure hours of a madhouse, though he couldn't see it. And he thought of his wife in every relation except the only fundamental one. He thought of her as a well-bred girl, as a wife, as a cultured person, as the mistress of a house, as a lady; but he never for a moment thought of her simply as a woman.

Then a fresh wave, a raging wave of humiliation, swept through his mind, and left nothing there but a personal sense of undeserved abasement. Why should he be mixed up with such a horrid exposure! It annihilated all the advantages of his well-ordered past, by a truth effective and unjust like a calumny—and the past was wasted. Its failure was disclosed—a distinct failure, on his part, to see, to guard, to understand. It could not be denied; it could not be explained away, hustled out of sight. He could not sit on it and look solemn. Now—if she had only died!

If she had only died! He was driven to envy such a respectable bereavement, and one so perfectly free from any taint of misfortune that even his best friend

or his best enemy would not have felt the slightest thrill
of exultation. No one would have cared. He sought
comfort in clinging to the contemplation of the only fact
of life that the resolute efforts of mankind had never
failed to disguise in the clatter and glamour of phrases.
And nothing lends itself more to lies than death. If
she had only died! Certain words would have been
said to him in a sad tone, and he, with proper fortitude,
would have made appropriate answers. There were
precedents for such an occasion. And no one would have
cared. If she had only died! The promises, the
terrors, the hopes of eternity, are the concern of the
corrupt dead; but the obvious sweetness of life belongs to living, healthy men. And life was his concern: that sane and gratifying existence untroubled by
too much love or by too much regret. She had in-
terfered with it; she had defaced it. And suddenly it
occurred to him he must have been mad to marry. It
was too much in the nature of giving yourself away, of
wearing—if for a moment—your heart on your sleeve.
But every one married. Was all mankind mad!

In the shock of that startling thought he looked up,
and saw to the left, to the right, in front, men sitting
far off in chairs and looking at him with wild eyes—
emissaries of a distracted mankind intruding to spy
upon his pain and his humiliation. It was not to be
borne. He rose quickly, and the others jumped up,
too, on all sides. He stood still in the middle of the
room as if discouraged by their vigilance. No escape!
He felt something akin to despair. Everybody must
know. The servants must know to-night. He ground
his teeth . . . And he had never noticed, never
guessed anything. Every one will know. He thought:
"The woman's a monster, but everybody will think me
a fool"; and standing still in the midst of severe walnut-

wood furniture, he felt such a tempest of anguish within him that he seemed to see himself rolling on the carpet, beating his head against the wall. He was disgusted with himself, with the loathsome rush of emotion breaking through all the reserves that guarded his manhood. Something unknown, withering and poisonous, had entered his life, passed near him, touched him, and he was deteriorating. He was appalled. What was it? She was gone. Why? His head was ready to burst with the endeavour to understand her act and his subtle horror of it. Everything was changed. Why? Only a woman gone, after all; and yet he had a vision, a vision quick and distinct as a dream: the vision of everything he had thought indestructible and safe in the world crashing down about him, like solid walls do before the fierce breath of a hurricane. He stared, shaking in every limb, while he felt the destructive breath, the mysterious breath, the breath of passion, stir the profound peace of the house. He looked round in fear. Yes. Crime may be forgiven; uncalculating sacrifice, blind trust, burning faith, other follies, may be turned to account; suffering, death itself, may with a grin or a frown be explained away; but passion is the unpardonable and secret infamy of our hearts, a thing to curse, to hide and to deny; a shameless and forlorn thing that tramples upon the smiling promises, that tears off the placid mask, that strips the body of life. And it had come to him! It had laid its unclean hand upon the spotless draperies of his existence, and he had to face it alone with all the world looking on. All the world! And he thought that even the bare suspicion of such an adversary within his house carried with it a taint and a condemnation. He put both his hands out as if to ward off the approach of a defiling truth; and, instantly, the appalled **conclave** of unreal men, standing about mutely beyond the clear lustre of mirrors, made at him the same gesture of rejection and horror.

He glanced vainly here and there, like a man looking in desperation for a weapon or for a hiding place, and understood at last that he was disarmed and cornered by the enemy that, without any squeamishness, would strike so as to lay open his heart. He could get help nowhere, or even take counsel with himself, because in the sudden shock of her desertion the sentiments which he knew that in fidelity to his bringing up, to his prejudices and his surroundings, he ought to experience, were so mixed up with the novelty of real feelings, of fundamental feelings that know nothing of creed, class, or education, that he was unable to distinguish clearly between what is and what ought to be; between the inexcusable truth and the valid pretences. And he knew instinctively that truth would be of no use to him. Some kind of concealment seemed a necessity because one cannot explain. Of course not! Who would listen? One had simply to be without stain and without reproach to keep one's place in the forefront of life.

He said to himself, "I must get over it the best I can," and began to walk up and down the room. What next? What ought to be done? He thought: "I will travel—no I won't. I shall face it out." And after that resolve he was greatly cheered by the reflection that it would be a mute and an easy part to play, for no one would be likely to converse with him about the abominable conduct of—that woman. He argued to himself that decent people—and he knew no others—did not care to talk about such indelicate affairs. She had gone off—with that unhealthy, fat ass of a journalist. Why? He had been all a husband ought to be. He

had given her a good position—she shared his prospects
—he had treated her invariably with great consideration. He reviewed his conduct with a kind of dismal
pride. It had been irreproachable. Then, why? For
love? Profanation! There could be no love there.
A shameful impulse of passion. Yes, passion. His
own wife! Good God! . . . And the indelicate
aspect of his domestic misfortune struck him with
such shame that, next moment, he caught himself in
the act of pondering absurdly over the notion whether
it would not be more dignified for him to induce a general belief that he had been in the habit of beating his
wife. Some fellows do . . . and anything would
be better than the filthy fact; for it was clear he had
lived with the root of it for five years—and it was too
shameful. Anything! Anything! Brutality . . .
But he gave it up directly, and began to think of the
Divorce Court. It did not present itself to him, notwithstanding his respect for law and usage, as a proper
refuge for dignified grief. It appeared rather as an
unclean and sinister cavern where men and women
are haled by adverse fate to writhe ridiculously in the
presence of uncompromising truth. It should not be
allowed. That woman! Five . . . years . . .
married five years . . . and never to see anything.
Not to the very last day . . . not till she coolly
went off. And he pictured to himself all the people he
knew engaged in speculating as to whether all that
time he had been blind, foolish, or infatuated. What
a woman! Blind! . . . Not at all. Could a
clean-minded man imagine such depravity? Evidently not. He drew a free breath. That was the
attitude to take; it was dignified enough; it gave him
the advantage, and he could not help perceiving that
it was moral. He yearned unaffectedly to see morality

(in his person) triumphant before the world. As to her—she would be forgotten. Let her be forgotten—buried in oblivion—lost! No one would allude . . . Refined people—and every man and woman he knew could be so described—had, of course, a horror of such topics. Had they? Oh, yes. No one would allude to her . . . in his hearing. He stamped his foot, tore the letter across, then again and again. The thought of sympathizing friends excited in him a fury of mistrust. He flung down the small bits of paper. They settled, fluttering at his feet, and looked very white on the dark carpet, like a scattered handful of snow-flakes.

This fit of hot anger was succeeded by a sudden sadness, by the darkening passage of a thought that ran over the scorched surface of his heart, like upon a barren plain, and after a fiercer assault of sunrays, the melancholy and cooling shadow of a cloud. He realized that he had had a shock—not a violent or rending blow, that can be seen, resisted, returned, forgotten, but a thrust, insidious and penetrating, that had stirred all those feelings, concealed and cruel, which the arts of the devil, the fears of mankind—God's infinite compassion, perhaps—keep chained deep down in the inscrutable twilight of our breasts. A dark curtain seemed to rise before him, and for less than a second he looked upon the mysterious universe of moral suffering. As a landscape is seen complete, and vast, and vivid, under a flash of lightning, so he could see disclosed in a moment all the immensity of pain that can be contained in one short moment of human thought. Then the curtain fell again, but his rapid vision left in Alvan Hervey's mind a trail of invincible sadness, a sense of loss and bitter solitude, as though he had been robbed and exiled. For a moment he ceased to be a member

of society with a position, a career, and a name attached to all this, like a descriptive label of some complicated compound. He was a simple human being
removed from the delightful world of crescents and
squares. He stood alone, naked and afraid, like
the first man on the first day of evil. There are in life
events, contacts, glimpses, that seem brutally to bring
all the past to a close. There is a shock and a crash,
as of a gate flung to behind one by the perfidious hand
of fate. Go and seek another paradise, fool or sage.
There is a moment of dumb dismay, and the wanderings must begin again; the painful explaining away of
facts, the feverish raking up of illusions, the cultivation
of a fresh crop of lies in the sweat of one's brow, to
sustain life, to make it supportable, to make it fair,
so as to hand intact to another generation of blind
wanderers the charming legend of a heartless country,
of a promised land, all flowers and blessings . . .

He came to himself with a slight start, and became
aware of an oppressive, crushing desolation. It was
only a feeling, it is true, but it produced on him a
physical effect, as though his chest had been squeezed
in a vice. He perceived himself so extremely forlorn
and lamentable, and was moved so deeply by the oppressive sorrow, that another turn of the screw, he felt,
would bring tears out of his eyes. He was deteriorating. Five years of life in common had appeased his
longing. Yes, long-time ago. The first five months
did that—but . . . There was the habit—the
habit of her person, of her smile, of her gestures, of her
voice, of her silence. She had a pure brow and good
hair. How utterly wretched all this was. Good hair
and fine eyes—remarkably fine. He was surprised by
the number of details that intruded upon his unwilling
memory. He could not help remembering her foot-

steps, the rustle of her dress, her way of holding her head, her decisive manner of saying "Alvan," the quiver of her nostrils when she was annoyed. All that had been so much his property, so intimately and specially his! He raged in a mournful, silent way, as he took stock of his losses. He was like a man counting the cost of an unlucky speculation—irritated, depressed —exasperated with himself and with others, with the fortunate, with the indifferent, with the callous; yet the wrong done him appeared so cruel that he would perhaps have dropped a tear over that spoliation if it had not been for his conviction that men do not weep. Foreigners do; they also kill sometimes in such circumstances. And to his horror he felt himself driven to regret almost that the usages of a society ready to forgive the shooting of a burglar forbade him, under the circumstances, even as much as a thought of murder. Nevertheless, he clenched his fists and set his teeth hard. And he was afraid at the same time. He was afraid with that penetrating faltering fear that seems, in the very middle of a beat, to turn one's heart into a handful of dust. The contamination of her crime spread out, tainted the universe, tainted himself; woke up all the dormant infamies of the world; caused a ghastly kind of clairvoyance in which he could see the towns and fields of the earth, its sacred places, its temples and its houses, peopled by monsters—by monsters of duplicity, lust, and murder. She was a monster—he himself was thinking monstrous thoughts . . . and yet he was like other people. How many men and women at this very moment were plunged in abominations—meditated crimes. It was frightful to think of. He remembered all the streets—the well-to-do streets he had passed on his way home; all the innumerable houses with closed doors and curtained windows. Each seemed now an abode of anguish and folly. And his thought, as if appalled, stood still, recalling with dismay the decorous and frightful silence that was like a conspiracy; the grim, impenetrable silence of miles of walls concealing passions, misery, thoughts of crime. Surely he was not the only man; his was not the only house . . . and yet no one knew—no one guessed. But he knew. He knew with unerring certitude that could not be deceived by the correct silence of walls, of closed doors, of curtained windows. He was beside himself with a despairing agitation, like a man informed of a deadly secret—the secret of a calamity threatening the safety of mankind—the sacredness, the peace of life.

He caught sight of himself in one of the looking-glasses. It was a relief. The anguish of his feeling had been so powerful that he more than half expected to see some distorted wild face there, and he was pleasantly surprised to see nothing of the kind. His aspect, at any rate, would let no one into the secret of his pain. He examined himself with attention. His trousers were turned up, and his boots a little muddy, but he looked very much as usual. Only his hair was slightly ruffled, and that disorder, somehow, was so suggestive of trouble that he went quickly to the table, and began to use the brushes, in an anxious desire to obliterate the compromising trace, that only vestige of his emotion. He brushed with care, watching the effect of his smoothing; and another face, slightly pale and more tense than was perhaps desirable, peered back at him from the toilet glass. He laid the brushes down, and was not satisfied. He took them up again and brushed, brushed mechanically—forgot himself in that occupation. The tumult of his thoughts ended in a sluggish flow of reflection, such as, after the outburst of a volcano, the almost imperceptible progress of a stream of lava, creeping languidly over a convulsed land and pitilessly obliterating any landmark left by the shock of the earthquake. It is a destructive but, by comparison, it is a peaceful phenomenon. Alvan Hervey was almost soothed by the deliberate pace of his thoughts. His moral landmarks were going one by one, consumed in the fire of his experience, buried in hot mud, in ashes. He was cooling—on the surface; but there was enough heat left somewhere to make him slap the brushes on the table, and turning away, say in a fierce whisper: "I wish him joy . . . Damn the woman."

He felt himself utterly corrupted by her wickedness, and the most significant symptom of his moral downfall was the bitter, acrid satisfaction with which he recognized it. He, deliberately, swore in his thoughts; he meditated sneers; he shaped in profound silence words of cynical unbelief, and his most cherished convictions stood revealed finally as the narrow prejudices of fools. A crowd of shapeless, unclean thoughts crossed his mind in a stealthy rush, like a band of veiled malefactors hastening to a crime. He put his hands deep into his pockets. He heard a faint ringing somewhere, and muttered to himself: "I am not the only one . . . not the only one." There was another ring. Front door!

His heart leaped up into his throat, and forthwith descended as low as his boots. A call! Who? Why? He wanted to rush out on the landing and shout to the servant: "Not at home! Gone away abroad!" . . . Any excuse. He could not face a visitor. Not this evening. No. To-morrow. . . . Before he could break out of the numbness that enveloped him like a sheet of lead, he heard far below, as if in the entrails of the earth, a door close heavily. The house vibrated to it more than to a clap of thunder. He stood still, wishing himself invisible. The room was very chilly. He did not think he would ever feel like that. But people must be met—they must be faced—talked to—smiled at. He heard another door, much nearer—the door of the drawing-room—being opened and flung to again. He imagined for a moment he would faint. How absurd! That kind of thing had to be gone through. A voice spoke. He could not catch the words. Then the voice spoke again, and footsteps were heard on the first floor landing. Hang it all! Was he to hear that voice and those footsteps whenever any one spoke or moved? He thought: "This is like being haunted—I suppose it will last for a week or so, at least. Till I forget. Forget! Forget!" Someone was coming up the second flight of stairs. Servant? He listened, then, suddenly, as though an incredible, frightful revelation had been shouted to him from a distance, he bellowed out in the empty room: "What! What!" in such a fiendish tone as to astonish himself. The footsteps stopped outside the door. He stood openmouthed, maddened and still, as if in the midst of a catastrophe. The door-handle rattled lightly. It seemed to him that the walls were coming apart, that the furniture swayed at him; the ceiling slanted queerly for a moment, a tall wardrobe tried to topple over. He caught hold of something and it was the back of a chair. So he had reeled against a chair! Oh! Confound it! He gripped hard.

The flaming butterfly poised between the jaws of the bronze dragon radiated a glare, a glare that seemed to leap up all at once into a crude, blinding fierceness, and made it difficult for him to distinguish plainly the figure of his wife standing upright with her back to the closed door. He looked at her and could not detect her breathing. The harsh and violent light was beating on her, and he was amazed to see her preserve so well the composure of her upright attitude in that scorching brilliance which, to his eyes, enveloped her like a hot and consuming mist. He would not have been surprised if she had vanished in it as suddenly as she had appeared. He stared and listened; listened for some sound, but the silence round him was absolute—as though he had in a moment grown completely deaf as well as dim-eyed. Then his hearing returned, preternaturally sharp. He heard the patter of a rain-shower on the window panes behind the lowered blinds, and below, far below, in the artificial abyss of the square, the deadened roll of wheels and the splashy trotting of a horse. He heard a groan also—very distinct—in the room—close to his ear.

He thought with alarm: "I must have made that noise myself;" and at the same instant the woman left the door, stepped firmly across the floor before him, and sat down in a chair. He knew that step. There was no doubt about it. She had come back! And he very nearly said aloud "Of course!"—such was his sudden and masterful perception of the indestructible character of her being. Nothing could destroy her—and nothing but his own destruction could keep her away. She was the incarnation of all the short moments which every man spares out of his life for dreams, for precious dreams that concrete the most cherished, the most profitable of his illusions. He peered at her with inward trepidation. She was mysterious, significant, full of obscure meaning—like a symbol. He peered, bending forward, as though he had been discovering about her things he had never seen before. Unconsciously he made a step towards her—then another. He saw her arm make an ample, decided movement— and he stopped. She had lifted her veil. It was like the lifting of a vizor.

The spell was broken. He experienced a shock as though he had been called out of a trance by the sudden noise of an explosion. It was even more startling and more distinct; it was an infinitely more intimate change, for he had the sensation of having come into this room only that very moment; of having returned from very far; he was made aware that some essential part of himself had in a flash returned into his body, returned finally from a fierce and lamentable region, from the dwelling-place of unveiled hearts. He woke up to an amazing infinity of contempt, to a droll bitterness of wonder, to a disenchanted conviction of safety. He had a glimpse of the irresistible force, and he saw also the barrenness of his convictions—of her convictions. It seemed to him that he could never make a mistake as long as he lived. It was morally impossible to go wrong. He was not elated by that certitude; he was dimly uneasy about its price; there was a chill as of death in this triumph of sound principles, in this victory snatched under the very shadow of disaster.

The last trace of his previous state of mind vanished, as the instantaneous and elusive trail of a bursting meteor vanishes on the profound blackness of the sky: it was the faint flicker of a painful thought, gone as soon as perceived, that nothing but her presence—after all— had the power to recall him to himself. He stared at her. She sat with her hands on her lap, looking down; and he noticed that her boots were dirty, her skirts wet and splashed, as though she had been driven back there by a blind fear through a waste of mud. He was indignant, amazed and shocked, but in a natural, healthy

way now; so that he could control those unprofitable
sentiments by the dictates of cautious self-restraint.
The light in the room had no unusual brilliance now;
it was a good light in which he could easily observe the
expression of her face. It was that of dull fatigue.
And the silence that surrounded them was the normal
silence of any quiet house, hardly disturbed by the
faint noises of a respectable quarter of the town. He
was very cool—and it was quite coolly that he thought
how much better it would be if neither of them ever
spoke again. She sat with closed lips, with an air of
lassitude in the stony forgetfulness of her pose, but
after a moment she lifted her drooping eyelids and met
his tense and inquisitive stare by a look that had all the
formless eloquence of a cry. It penetrated, it stirred
without informing; it was the very essence of anguish
stripped of words that can be smiled at, argued away,
shouted down, disdained. It was anguish naked and
unashamed, the bare pain of existence let loose upon
the world in the fleeting unreserve of a look that had
in it an immensity of fatigue, the scornful sincerity,
the black impudence of an extorted confession. Alvan
Hervey was seized with wonder, as though he had seen
something inconceivable; and some obscure part of his
being was ready to exclaim with him: "I would never
have believed it!" but an instantaneous revulsion of
wounded susceptibilities checked the unfinished thought.

He felt full of rancorous indignation against the
woman who could look like this at one. This look
probed him; it tampered with him. It was dangerous
to one as would be a hint of unbelief whispered by a
priest in the august decorum of a temple; and at the
same time it was impure, it was disturbing, like a cynical
consolation muttered in the dark, tainting the sorrow,
corroding the thought, poisoning the heart. He

wanted to ask her furiously: "Who do you take me for? How dare you look at me like this?" He felt himself helpless before the hidden meaning of that look; he resented it with pained and futile violence as an injury so secret that it could never, never be redressed. His wish was to crush her by a single sentence. He was stainless. Opinion was on his side; morality, men and gods were on his side; law, conscience—all the world! She had nothing but that look. And he could only say:

"How long do you intend to stay here?"

Her eyes did not waver, her lips remained closed; and for any effect of his words he might have spoken to a dead woman, only that this one breathed quickly. He was profoundly disappointed by what he had said. It was a great deception, something in the nature of treason. He had deceived himself. It should have been altogether different—other words—another sensation. And before his eyes, so fixed that at times they saw nothing, she sat apparently as unconscious as though she had been alone, sending that look of brazen confession straight at him—with an air of staring into empty space. He said significantly:

"Must I go then?" And he knew he meant nothing of what he implied.

One of her hands on her lap moved slightly as though his words had fallen there and she had thrown them off on the floor. But her silence encouraged him. Possibly it meant remorse—perhaps fear. Was she thunderstruck by his attitude? . . . Her eyelids dropped. He seemed to understand ever so much—everything! Very well—but she must be made to suffer. It was due to him. He understood everything, yet he judged it indispensable to say with an obvious affectation of civility:

"I don't understand—be so good as to . . ."

She stood up. For a second he believed she intended to go away, and it was as though someone had jerked a string attached to his heart. It hurt. He remained open-mouthed and silent. But she made an irresolute step towards him, and instinctively he moved aside. They stood before one another, and the fragments of the torn letter lay between them—at their feet—like an insurmountable obstacle, like a sign of eternal separation! Around them three other couples stood still and face to face, as if waiting for a signal to begin some action—a struggle, a dispute, or a dance.

She said: "Don't—Alvan!" and there was something that resembled a warning in the pain of her tone. He narrowed his eyes as if trying to pierce her with his gaze. Her voice touched him. He had aspirations after magnanimity, generosity, superiority—interrupted, however, by flashes of indignation and anxiety—frightful anxiety to know how far she had gone. She looked down at the torn paper. Then she looked up, and their eyes met again, remained fastened together, like an unbreakable bond, like a clasp of eternal complicity; and the decorous silence, the pervading quietude of the house which enveloped this meeting of their glances became for a moment inexpressibly vile, for he was afraid she would say too much and make magnanimity impossible, while behind the profound mournfulness of her face there was a regret—a regret of things done—the regret of delay—the thought that if she had only turned back a week sooner—a day sooner—only an hour sooner. . . . They were afraid to hear again the sound of their voices; they did not know what they might say—perhaps something that could not be recalled; and words are more terrible than facts. But the tricky fatality that lurks in

obscure impulses spoke through Alvan Hervey's lips
suddenly; and he heard his own voice with the excited
and sceptical curiosity with which one listens to actors'
voices speaking on the stage in the strain of a poignant
situation.

"If you have forgotten anything . . . of course
. . . I . . ."

Her eyes blazed at him for an instant; her lips
trembled—and then she also became the mouth-piece
of the mysterious force forever hovering near us; of
that perverse inspiration, wandering capricious and uncontrollable, like a gust of wind.

"What is the good of this, Alvan? . . . You
know why I came back. . . . You know that I
could not . . ."

He interrupted her with irritation.

"Then! what's this?" he asked, pointing downwards
at the torn letter.

"That's a mistake," she said hurriedly, in a muffled
voice.

This answer amazed him. He remained speechless,
staring at her. He had half a mind to burst into a
laugh. It ended in a smile as involuntary as a grimace
of pain.

"A mistake . . ." he began, slowly, and then
found himself unable to say another word.

"Yes . . . it was honest," she said very low, as
if speaking to the memory of a feeling in a remote past.

He exploded.

"Curse your honesty! . . . Is there any honesty
in all this! . . . When did you begin to be honest?
Why are you here? What are you now? . . . Still
honest? . . ."

He walked at her, raging, as if blind; during these
three quick strides he lost touch of the material world

and was whirled interminably through a kind of empty
universe made up of nothing but fury and anguish, till
he came suddenly upon her face—very close to his.
He stopped short, and all at once seemed to remember
something heard ages ago.

"You don't know the meaning of the word," he
shouted.

She did not flinch. He perceived with fear that
everything around him was still. She did not move
a hair's breadth; his own body did not stir. An im-
perturbable calm enveloped their two motionless
figures, the house, the town, all the world—and the
trifling tempest of his feelings. The violence of
the short tumult within him had been such as could
well have shattered all creation; and yet nothing
was changed. He faced his wife in the familiar room
in his own house. It had not fallen. And right and
left all the innumerable dwellings, standing shoulder
to shoulder, had resisted the shock of his passion, had
presented, unmoved, to the loneliness of his trouble,
the grim silence of walls, the impenetrable and polished
discretion of closed doors and curtained windows. Immobility and silence pressed on him, assailed him, like
two accomplices of the immovable and mute woman
before his eyes. He was suddenly vanquished. He
was shown his impotence. He was soothed by the
breath of a corrupt resignation coming to him through
the subtle irony of the surrounding peace.

He said with villainous composure:

"At any rate it isn't enough for me. I want to know
more—if you're going to stay."

"There is nothing more to tell," she answered, sadly.

It struck him as so very true that he did not say
anything. She went on:

"You wouldn't understand. . . ."

"No?" he said, quietly. He held himself tight not to burst into howls and imprecations.

"I tried to be faithful . . ." she began again.

"And this?" he exclaimed, pointing at the fragments of her letter.

"This—this is a failure," she said.

"I should think so," he muttered, bitterly.

"I tried to be faithful to myself—Alvan—and . . . and honest to you. . . ."

"If you had tried to be faithful to me it would have been more to the purpose," he interrupted, angrily. "I've been faithful to you—and you have spoiled my life—both our lives . . ." Then after a pause the unconquerable preoccupation of self came out, and he raised his voice to ask resentfully, "And, pray, for how long have you been making a fool of me?"

She seemed horribly shocked by that question. He did not wait for an answer, but went on moving about all the time; now and then coming up to her, then wandering off restlessly to the other end of the room.

"I want to know. Everybody knows, I suppose, but myself—and that's your honesty!"

"I have told you there is nothing to know," she said, speaking unsteadily as if in pain. "Nothing of what you suppose. You don't understand me. This letter is the beginning—and the end."

"The end—this thing has no end," he clamoured, unexpectedly. "Can't you understand that? I can . . . The beginning . . ."

He stopped and looked into her eyes with concentrated intensity, with a desire to see, to penetrate, to understand, that made him positively hold his breath till he gasped.

"By Heavens!" he said, standing perfectly still in a peering attitude and within less than a foot from her.

"By Heavens!" he repeated, slowly, and in a tone whose involuntary strangeness was a complete mystery to himself. "By Heavens—I could believe you—I could believe anything—now!"

He turned short on his heel and began to walk up and down the room with an air of having disburdened himself of the final pronouncement of his life—of having said something on which he would not go back, even if he could. She remained as if rooted to the carpet. Her eyes followed the restless movements of the man, who avoided looking at her. Her wide stare clung to him, inquiring, wondering and doubtful.

"But the fellow was forever sticking in here," he burst out, distractedly. "He made love to you, I suppose—and, and . . ." He lowered his voice. "And —you let him."

"And I let him," she murmured, catching his intonation, so that her voice sounded unconscious, sounded far off and slavish, like an echo.

He said twice, "You! You!" violently, then calmed down. "What could you see in the fellow?" he asked, with unaffected wonder. "An effeminate, fat ass. What could you . . . Weren't you happy? Didn't you have all you wanted? Now—frankly; did I deceive your expectations in any way? Were you disappointed with our position—or with our prospects— perhaps? You know you couldn't be—they are much better than you could hope for when you married me. . . ."

He forgot himself so far as to gesticulate a little while he went on with animation:

"What could you expect from such a fellow? He's an outsider—a rank outsider. . . . If it hadn't been for my money . . . do you hear? . . . for my money, he wouldn't know where to turn. His

people won't have anything to do with him. The
fellow's no class—no class at all. He's useful, certainly,
that's why I . . . I thought you had enough
intelligence to see it. . . . And you . . . No!
It's incredible! What did he tell you? Do you care
for no one's opinion—is there no restraining influence
in the world for you—women? Did you ever give me a
thought? I tried to be a good husband. Did I fail?
Tell me—what have I done?"

Carried away by his feelings he took his head in both
his hands and repeated wildly:

"What have I done? . . . Tell me!
What? . . ."

"Nothing," she said.

"Ah! You see . . . you can't . . ." he
began, triumphantly, walking away; then suddenly, as
though he had been flung back at her by something
invisible he had met, he spun round and shouted with
exasperation:

"What on earth did you expect me to do?"

Without a word she moved slowly towards the table,
and, sitting down, leaned on her elbow, shading her
eyes with her hand. All that time he glared at her
watchfully as if expecting every moment to find in
her deliberate movements an answer to his question.
But he could not read anything, he could gather no
hint of her thought. He tried to suppress his desire
to shout, and after waiting awhile, said with incisive
scorn:

"Did you want me to write absurd verses; to sit and
look at you for hours—to talk to you about your soul?
You ought to have known I wasn't that sort. . . .
I had something better to do. But if you think I was
totally blind . . ."

He perceived in a flash that he could remember an

infinity of enlightening occurrences. He could recall ever so many distinct occasions when he came upon them; he remembered the absurdly interrupted gesture of his fat, white hand, the rapt expression of her face, the glitter of unbelieving eyes; snatches of incomprehensible conversations not worth listening to, silences that had meant nothing at the time and seemed now illuminating like a burst of sunshine. He remembered all that. He had not been blind. Oh! No! And to know this was an exquisite relief: it brought back all his composure.

"I thought it beneath me to suspect you," he said, loftily.

The sound of that sentence evidently possessed some magical power, because, as soon as he had spoken, he felt wonderfully at ease; and directly afterwards he experienced a flash of joyful amazement at the discovery that he could be inspired to such noble and truthful utterance. He watched the effect of his words. They caused her to glance at him quickly over her shoulder. He caught a glimpse of wet eyelashes, of a red cheek with a tear running down swiftly; and then she turned away again and sat as before, covering her face with her hands.

"You ought to be perfectly frank with me," he said, slowly.

"You know everything," she answered, indistinctly, through her fingers.

"This letter. . . . Yes . . . but . . ."

"And I came back," she exclaimed in a stifled voice; "you know everything."

"I am glad of it—for your sake," he said with impressive gravity. He listened to himself with solemn emotion. It seemed to him that something inexpressibly momentous was in progress within the room, that

every word and every gesture had the importance of
events preordained from the beginning of all things, and
summing up in their finality the whole purpose of
creation.

"For your sake," he repeated.

Her shoulders shook as though she had been sobbing,
and he forgot himself in the contemplation of her hair.
Suddenly he gave a start, as if waking up, and asked
very gently and not much above a whisper—

"Have you been meeting him often?"

"Never!" she cried into the palms of her hands.

This answer seemed for a moment to take from him
the power of speech. His lips moved for some time
before any sound came.

"You preferred to make love here—under my very
nose," he said, furiously. He calmed down instantly,
and felt regretfully uneasy, as though he had let himself down in her estimation by that outburst. She
rose, and with her hand on the back of the chair confronted him with eyes that were perfectly dry now.
There was a red spot on each of her cheeks.

"When I made up my mind to go to him—I wrote,"
she said.

"But you didn't go to him," he took up in the same
tone. "How far did you go? What made you come
back?"

"I didn't know myself," she murmured. Nothing
of her moved but her lips. He fixed her sternly.

"Did he expect this? Was he waiting for you?" he
asked.

She answered him by an almost imperceptible nod,
and he continued to look at her for a good while without making a sound. Then, at last—

"And I suppose he is waiting yet?" he asked, quickly.

Again she seemed to nod at him. For some reason

he felt he must know the time. He consulted his watch gloomily. Half-past seven.

"Is he?" he muttered, putting the watch in his pocket. He looked up at her, and, as if suddenly overcome by a sense of sinister fun, gave a short, harsh laugh, directly repressed.

"No! It's the most unheard! . . ." he mumbled while she stood before him biting her lower lip, as if plunged in deep thought. He laughed again in one low burst that was as spiteful as an imprecation. He did not know why he felt such an overpowering and sudden distaste for the facts of existence—for facts in general —such an immense disgust at the thought of all the many days already lived through. He was wearied. Thinking seemed a labour beyond his strength. He said—

"You deceived me—now you make a fool of him . . . It's awful! Why?"

"I deceived myself!" she exclaimed.

"Oh! Nonsense!" he said, impatiently.

"I am ready to go if you wish it," she went on, quickly. "It was due to you—to be told—to know. No! I could not!" she cried, and stood still wringing her hands stealthily.

"I am glad you repented before it was too late," he said in a dull tone and looking at his boots. "I am glad . . . some spark of better feeling," he muttered, as if to himself. He lifted up his head after a moment of brooding silence. "I am glad to see that there is some sense of decency left in you," he added a little louder. Looking at her he appeared to hesitate, as if estimating the possible consequences of what he wished to say, and at last blurted out—

"After all, I loved you. . . ."

"I did not know," she whispered.

"Good God!" he cried. "Why do you imagine I married you?"

The indelicacy of his obtuseness angered her.

"Ah—why?" she said through her teeth.

He appeared overcome with horror, and watched her lips intently as though in fear.

"I imagined many things," she said, slowly, and paused. He watched, holding his breath. At last she went on musingly, as if thinking aloud, "I tried to understand. I tried honestly. . . . Why? . . . To do the usual thing—I suppose. . . . To please yourself."

He walked away smartly, and when he came back, close to her, he had a flushed face.

"You seemed pretty well pleased, too—at the time," he hissed, with scathing fury. "I needn't ask whether you loved me."

"I know now I was perfectly incapable of such a thing," she said, calmly, "If I had, perhaps you would not have married me."

"It's very clear I would not have done it if I had known you—as I know you now."

He seemed to see himself proposing to her—ages ago. They were strolling up the slope of a lawn. Groups of people were scattered in sunshine. The shadows of leafy boughs lay still on the short grass. The coloured sunshades far off, passing between trees, resembled deliberate and brilliant butterflies moving without a flutter. Men smiling amiably, or else very grave, within the impeccable shelter of their black coats, stood by the side of women who, clustered in clear summer toilettes, recalled all the fabulous tales of enchanted gardens where animated flowers smile at bewitched knights. There was a sumptuous serenity in it all, a thin, vibrating excitement, the perfect security, as of an invincible ignorance, that evoked within him a transcendent belief in felicity as the lot of all mankind, a recklessly picturesque desire to get promptly something for himself only, out of that splendour unmarred by any shadow of a thought. The girl walked by his side across an open space; no one was near, and suddenly he stood still, as if inspired, and spoke. He remembered looking at her pure eyes, at her candid brow; he remembered glancing about quickly to see if they were being observed, and thinking that nothing could go wrong in a world of so much charm, purity, and distinction. He was proud of it. He was one of its makers, of its possessors, of its guardians, of its extollers. He wanted to grasp it solidly, to get as much gratification as he could out of it; and in view of its incomparable quality, of its unstained atmosphere, of its nearness to the heaven of its choice, this gust of brutal desire seemed the most noble of aspirations. In a second he lived again through all these moments, and then all the pathos of his failure presented itself to him with such vividness that there was a suspicion of tears in his tone when he said almost unthinkingly, "My God! I did love you!"

She seemed touched by the emotion of his voice. Her lips quivered a little, and she made one faltering step towards him, putting out her hands in a beseeching gesture, when she perceived, just in time, that being absorbed by the tragedy of his life he had absolutely forgotten her very existence. She stopped, and her outstretched arms fell slowly. He, with his features distorted by the bitterness of his thought, saw neither her movement nor her gesture. He stamped his foot in vexation, rubbed his head—then exploded.

"What the devil am I to do now?"

He was still again. She seemed to understand, and moved to the door firmly.

"It's very simple—I'm going," she said aloud.

At the sound of her voice he gave a start of surprise, looked at her wildly, and asked in a piercing tone—

"You. . . . Where? To him?"

"No—alone—good-bye."

The door-handle rattled under her groping hand as though she had been trying to get out of some dark place.

"No—stay!" he cried.

She heard him faintly. He saw her shoulder touch the lintel of the door. She swayed as if dazed. There was less than a second of suspense while they both felt as if poised on the very edge of moral annihilation, ready to fall into some devouring nowhere. Then, almost simultaneously, he shouted, "Come back!" and she let go the handle of the door. She turned round in peaceful desperation like one who deliberately has thrown away the last chance of life; and, for a moment, the room she faced appeared terrible, and dark, and safe—like a grave.

He said, very hoarse and abrupt: "It can't end like this. . . . Sit down;" and while she crossed the room again to the low-backed chair before the dressing-table, he opened the door and put his head out to look and listen. The house was quiet. He came back pacified, and asked—

"Do you speak the truth?"

She nodded.

"You have lived a lie, though," he said, suspiciously.

"Ah! You made it so easy," she answered.

"You reproach me—me!"

"How could I?" she said; "I would have you no other—now."

"What do you mean by . . ." he began, then checked himself, and without waiting for an answer went on, "I won't ask any questions. Is this letter the worst of it?"

She had a nervous movement of her hands.

"I must have a plain answer," he said, hotly.

"Then, no! The worst is my coming back."

There followed a period of dead silence, during which they exchanged searching glances.

He said authoritatively—

"You don't know what you are saying. Your mind is unhinged. You are beside yourself, or you would not say such things. You can't control yourself. Even in your remorse . . ." He paused a moment, then said with a doctoral air: "Self-restraint is everything in life, you know. It's happiness, it's dignity . . . it's everything."

She was pulling nervously at her handkerchief while he went on watching anxiously to see the effect of his words. Nothing satisfactory happened. Only, as he began to speak again, she covered her face with both her hands.

"You see where the want of self-restraint leads to. Pain—humiliation—loss of respect—of friends, of everything that ennobles life, that . . . All kinds of horrors," he concluded, abruptly.

She made no stir. He looked at her pensively for some time as though he had been concentrating the melancholy thoughts evoked by the sight of that abased woman. His eyes became fixed and dull. He was profoundly penetrated by the solemnity of the moment; he felt deeply the greatness of the occasion. And more than ever the walls of his house seemed to enclose the sacredness of ideals to which he was about to offer a magnificent sacrifice. He was the high

priest of that temple, the severe guardian of formulas,
of rites, of the pure ceremonial concealing the black
doubts of life. And he was not alone. Other men, too
—the best of them—kept watch and ward by the
hearthstones that were the altars of that profitable persuasion. He understood confusedly that he was part
of an immense and beneficent power, which had a
reward ready for every discretion. He dwelt within
the invincible wisdom of silence; he was protected by
an indestructible faith that would last forever, that
would withstand unshaken all the assaults—the loud
execrations of apostates, and the secret weariness of its
confessors! He was in league with a universe of untold
advantages. He represented the moral strength of a
beautiful reticence that could vanquish all the deplorable crudities of life—fear, disaster, sin—even death
itself. It seemed to him he was on the point of sweeping triumphantly away all the illusory mysteries of
existence. It was simplicity itself.

"I hope you see now the folly—the utter folly of
wickedness," he began in a dull, solemn manner. "You
must respect the conditions of your life or lose all it
can give you. All! Everything!"

He waved his arm once, and three exact replicas of
his face, of his clothes, of his dull severity, of his solemn
grief, repeated the wide gesture that in its comprehen-
sive sweep indicated an infinity of moral sweetness,
embraced the walls, the hangings, the whole house, all
the crowd of houses outside, all the flimsy and inscrutable graves of the living, with their doors numbered
like the doors of prison-cells, and as impenetrable as the
granite of tombstones.

"Yes! Restraint, duty, fidelity—unswerving fidelity
to what is expected of you. This—only this—secures
the reward, the peace. Everything else we should

labour to subdue—to destroy. It's misfortune; it's disease. It is terrible—terrible. We must not know anything about it—we needn't. It is our duty to ourselves—to others. You do not live all alone in the world—and if you have no respect for the dignity of life, others have. Life is a serious matter. If you don't conform to the highest standards you are no one—it's a kind of death. Didn't this occur to you? You've only to look round you to see the truth of what I am saying. Did you live without noticing anything, without understanding anything? From a child you had examples before your eyes—you could see daily the beauty, the blessings of morality, of principles. . . ."

His voice rose and fell pompously in a strange chant. His eyes were still, his stare exalted and sullen; his face was set, was hard, was woodenly exulting over the grim inspiration that secretly possessed him, seethed within him, lifted him up into a stealthy frenzy of belief. Now and then he would stretch out his right arm over her head, as it were, and he spoke down at that sinner from a height, and with a sense of avenging virtue, with a profound and pure joy as though he could from his steep pinnacle see every weighty word strike and hurt like a punishing stone.

"Rigid principles—adherence to what is right," he finished after a pause.

"What is right?" she said, distinctly, without uncovering her face.

"Your mind is diseased!" he cried, upright and austere. "Such a question is rot—utter rot. Look round you—there's your answer, if you only care to see. Nothing that outrages the received beliefs can be right. Your conscience tells you that. They are the received beliefs because they are the best, the noblest, the only possible. They survive. . . ."

He could not help noticing with pleasure the philosophic breadth of his view, but he could not pause to enjoy it, for his inspiration, the call of august truth, carried him on.

"You must respect the moral foundations of a society that has made you what you are. Be true to it. That's duty—that's honour—that's honesty."

He felt a great glow within him, as though he had swallowed something hot. He made a step nearer. She sat up and looked at him with an ardour of expectation that stimulated his sense of the supreme importance of that moment. And as if forgetting himself he raised his voice very much.

"'What's right?' you ask me. Think only. What would you have been if you had gone off with that infernal vagabond? . . . What would you have been? . . . You! My wife! . . ."

He caught sight of himself in the pier glass, drawn up to his full height, and with a face so white that his eyes, at the distance, resembled the black cavities in a skull. He saw himself as if about to launch imprecations, with arms uplifted above her bowed head. He was ashamed of that unseemly posture, and put his hands in his pockets hurriedly. She murmured faintly, as if to herself—

"Ah! What am I now?"

"As it happens you are still Mrs. Alvan Hervey—uncommonly lucky for you, let me tell you," he said in a conversational tone. He walked up to the furthest corner of the room, and, turning back, saw her sitting very upright, her hands clasped on her lap, and with a lost, unswerving gaze of her eyes which stared unwinking like the eyes of the blind, at the crude gas flame, blazing and still, between the jaws of the bronze dragon.

He came up quite close to her, and straddling his legs a little, stood looking down at her face for some time without taking his hands out of his pockets. He seemed to be turning over in his mind a heap of words, piecing his next speech out of an overpowering abundance of thoughts.

"You've tried me to the utmost," he said at last; and as soon as he said these words he lost his moral footing, and felt himself swept away from his pinnacle by a flood of passionate resentment against the bungling creature that had come so near to spoiling his life. "Yes; I've been tried more than any man ought to be," he went on with righteous bitterness. "It was unfair. What possessed you to? . . .   What possessed you? . . . Write such a . . . After five years of perfect happiness! 'Pon my word, no one would believe. . . . Didn't you feel you couldn't? Because you couldn't . . . it was impossible—you know. Wasn't it? Think. Wasn't it?"

"It was impossible," she whispered, obediently.

This submissive assent given with such readiness did not soothe him, did not elate him; it gave him, inexplicably, that sense of terror we experience when in the midst of conditions we had learned to think absolutely safe we discover all at once the presence of a near and unsuspected danger. It was impossible, of course! He knew it. She knew it. She confessed it. It was impossible! That man knew it, too—as well as any one; couldn't help knowing it. And yet those two had been engaged in a conspiracy against his peace—in a criminal enterprise for which there could be no sanction of belief within themselves. There could not be! There could not be! And yet how near to . . .   With a short thrill he saw himself an exiled forlorn figure in a realm of ungovernable, of unrestrained folly. Nothing could be foreseen, foretold—guarded against. And the sensation was intolerable, had something of the withering horror that may be conceived as following upon the utter extinction of all hope. In the flash of thought the dishonouring episode seemed to disengage itself from everything actual, from earthly conditions, and even from earthly suffering; it became purely a terrifying knowledge, an annihilating knowledge of a blind and infernal force. Something desperate and vague, a flicker of an insane desire to abase himself before the mysterious impulses of evil, to ask for mercy in some way, passed through his mind; and then came the idea, the persuasion, the certitude, that the evil must be forgotten—must be resolutely ignored to make life possible; that the knowledge must be kept out of mind, out of sight, like the knowledge of certain death is kept out of the daily existence of men. He stiffened himself inwardly for the effort, and next moment it appeared very easy, amazingly feasible, if one only kept strictly to facts, gave one's mind to their perplexities and not to their meaning. Becoming conscious of a long silence, he cleared his throat warningly, and said in a steady voice—

"I am glad you feel this . . . uncommonly glad . . . you felt this in time. For, don't you see . . ." Unexpectedly he hesitated.

"Yes . . . I see," she murmured.

"Of course you would," he said, looking at the carpet and speaking like one who thinks of something else. He lifted his head. "I cannot believe—even after this— even after this—that you are altogether—altogether . . . other than what I thought you. It seems impossible—to me."

"And to me," she breathed out.

"Now—yes," he said, "but this morning? And tomorrow? . . . This is what . . ."

He started at the drift of his words and broke off abruptly. Every train of thought seemed to lead into the hopeless realm of ungovernable folly, to recall the knowledge and the terror of forces that must be ignored. He said rapidly—

"My position is very painful—difficult . . . I feel . . ."

He looked at her fixedly with a pained air, as though frightfully oppressed by a sudden inability to express his pent-up ideas.

"I am ready to go," she said very low. "I have forfeited everything . . . to learn . . . to learn . . ."

Her chin fell on her breast; her voice died out in a sigh. He made a slight gesture of impatient assent.

"Yes! Yes! It's all very well . . . of course. Forfeited—ah! Morally forfeited—only morally forfeited . . . if I am to believe you . . ."

She startled him by jumping up.

"Oh! I believe, I believe," he said, hastily, and she sat down as suddenly as she had got up. He went on gloomily—

"I've suffered—I suffer now. You can't understand how much. So much that when you propose a parting I almost think. . . . But no. There is duty. You've forgotten it; I never did. Before heaven, I never did. But in a horrid exposure like this the judgment of mankind goes astray—at least for a time. You see, you and I—at least I feel that—you and I are one before the world. It is as it should be. The world is right—in the main—or else it couldn't be—couldn't be—what it is. And we are part of it. We have our duty to—to our fellow beings who don't want to . . . to. . . . er."

He stammered. She looked up at him with wide

eyes, and her lips were slightly parted. He went on mumbling—

". . . Pain. . . . Indignation. . . . Sure to misunderstand. I've suffered enough. And if there has been nothing irreparable—as you assure me . . . then . . ."

"Alvan!" she cried.

"What?" he said, morosely. He gazed down at her for a moment with a sombre stare, as one looks at ruins, at the devastation of some natural disaster.

"'Then," he continued after a short pause, "the best thing is . . . the best for us . . . for every one. . . . Yes . . . least pain—most unselfish. . . ." His voice faltered, and she heard only detached words. ". . . Duty. . . . Burden. . . . Ourselves. . . . Silence."

A moment of perfect stillness ensued.

"This is an appeal I am making to your conscience," he said, suddenly, in an explanatory tone, "not to add to the wretchedness of all this: to try loyally and help me to live it down somehow. Without any reservations—you know. Loyally! You can't deny I've been cruelly wronged and—after all—my affection deserves . . ." He paused with evident anxiety to hear her speak.

"I make no reservations," she said, mournfully. "How could I? I found myself out and came back to . . ." her eyes flashed scornfully for an instant ". . . to what—to what you propose. You see . . . I . . . I can be trusted . . . now."

He listened to every word with profound attention, and when she ceased seemed to wait for more.

"Is that all you've got to say?" he asked.

She was startled by his tone, and said faintly—

"I spoke the truth. What more can I say?"

"Confound it! You might say something human," he burst out. "It isn't being truthful; it's being brazen—if you want to know. Not a word to show you feel your position, and—and mine. Not a single word of acknowledgment, or regret—or remorse . . . or . . . something."

"Words!" she whispered in a tone that irritated him. He stamped his foot.

"This is awful!" he exclaimed. "Words? Yes, words. Words mean something—yes—they do—for all this infernal affectation. They mean something to me—to everybody—to you. What the devil did you use to express those sentiments—sentiments—pah!— which made you forget me, duty, shame!" . . . He foamed at the mouth while she stared at him, appalled by this sudden fury. "Did you two talk only with your eyes?" he spluttered savagely. She rose.

"I can't bear this," she said, trembling from head to foot. "I am going."

They stood facing one another for a moment.

"Not you," he said, with conscious roughness, and began to walk up and down the room. She remained very still with an air of listening anxiously to her own heart-beats, then sank down on the chair slowly, and sighed, as if giving up a task beyond her strength.

"You misunderstand everything I say," he began quietly, "but I prefer to think that—just now—you are not accountable for your actions." He stopped again before her. "Your mind is unhinged," he said, with unction. "To go now would be adding crime—yes, crime—to folly. I'll have no scandal in my life, no matter what's the cost. And why? You are sure to misunderstand me—but I'll tell you. As a matter of duty. Yes. But you're sure to misunderstand me—

recklessly. Women always do—they are too—too narrow-minded."

He waited for a while, but she made no sound, didn't even look at him; he felt uneasy, painfully uneasy, like a man who suspects he is unreasonably mistrusted. To combat that exasperating sensation he recommenced talking very fast. The sound of his words excited his thoughts, and in the play of darting thoughts he had glimpses now and then of the inexpugnable rock of his convictions, towering in solitary grandeur above the unprofitable waste of errors and passions.

"For it is self-evident," he went on with anxious vivacity, "it is self-evident that, on the highest ground we haven't the right—no, we haven't the right to intrude our miseries upon those who—who naturally expect better things from us. Every one wishes his own life and the life around him to be beautiful and pure. Now, a scandal amongst people of our position is disastrous for the morality—a fatal influence—don't you see—upon the general tone of the class—very important—the most important, I verily believe, in—in the community. I feel this—profoundly. This is the broad view. In time you'll give me . . . when you become again the woman I loved—and trusted. . . ."

He stopped short, as though unexpectedly suffocated, then in a completely changed voice said, "For I did love and trust you"—and again was silent for a moment. She put her handkerchief to her eyes.

"You'll give me credit for—for—my motives. It's mainly loyalty to—to the larger conditions of our life—where you—you! of all women—failed. One doesn't usually talk like this—of course—but in this case you'll admit . . . And consider—the innocent suffer with the guilty. The world is pitiless in its judgments. Unfortunately there are always those in it who are only too eager to misunderstand. Before you and before my conscience I am guiltless, but any—any disclosure would impair my usefulness in the sphere—in the larger sphere in which I hope soon to . . . I believe you fully shared my views in that matter—I don't want to say any more . . . on—on that point—but, believe me, true unselfishness is to bear one's burdens in—in silence. The ideal must—must be preserved—for others, at least. It's clear as daylight. If I've a—a loathsome sore, to gratuitously display it would be abominable—abominable! And often in life—in the highest conception of life—outspokenness in certain circumstances is nothing less than criminal. Temptation, you know, excuses no one. There is no such thing really if one looks steadily to one's welfare—which is grounded in duty. But there are the weak." . . . His tone became ferocious for an instant . . . "And there are the fools and the envious—especially for people in our position. I am guiltless of this terrible—terrible . . . estrangement; but if there has been nothing irreparable." . . . Something gloomy, like a deep shadow passed over his face. . . . "Nothing irreparable—you see even now I am ready to trust you implicitly—then our duty is clear."

He looked down. A change came over his expression and straightway from the outward impetus of his loquacity he passed into the dull contemplation of all the appeasing truths that, not without some wonder, he had so recently been able to discover within himself. During this profound and soothing communion with his innermost beliefs he remained staring at the carpet, with a portentously solemn face and with a dull vacuity of eyes that seemed to gaze into the blankness of an empty hole. Then, without stirring in the least, he continued:

"Yes. Perfectly clear. I've been tried to the utmost, and I can't pretend that, for a time, the old feelings—the old feelings are not. . . ." He sighed. . . . "But I forgive you. . . ."

She made a slight movement without uncovering her eyes. In his profound scrutiny of the carpet he noticed nothing. And there was silence, silence within and silence without, as though his words had stilled the beat and tremor of all the surrounding life, and the house had stood alone—the only dwelling upon a deserted earth.

He lifted his head and repeated solemnly:

"I forgive you . . . from a sense of duty—and in the hope . . ."

He heard a laugh, and it not only interrupted his words but also destroyed the peace of his self-absorption with the vile pain of a reality intruding upon the beauty of a dream. He couldn't understand whence the sound came. He could see, foreshortened, the tear-stained, dolorous face of the woman stretched out, and with her head thrown over the back of the seat. He thought the piercing noise was a delusion. But another shrill peal followed by a deep sob and succeeded by another shriek of mirth positively seemed to tear him out from where he stood. He bounded to the door. It was closed. He turned the key and thought: that's no good. . . . "Stop this!" he cried, and perceived with alarm that he could hardly hear his own voice in the midst of her screaming. He darted back with the idea of stifling that unbearable noise with his hands, but stood still distracted, finding himself as unable to touch her as though she had been on fire. He shouted, "Enough of this!" like men shout in the tumult of a riot, with a red face and starting eyes; then, as if swept away before another burst of laughter, he disappeared in a flash out of three looking-glasses, vanished suddenly from before her. For a time the woman gasped and laughed at no one in the luminous stillness of the empty room.

He reappeared, striding at her, and with a tumbler of water in his hand. He stammered: "Hysterics— Stop—They will hear—Drink this." She laughed at the ceiling. "Stop this!" he cried. "Ah!"

He flung the water in her face, putting into the action all the secret brutality of his spite, yet still felt that it would have been perfectly excusable—in any one—to send the tumbler after the water. He restrained himself, but at the same time was so convinced nothing could stop the horror of those mad shrieks that, when the first sensation of relief came, it did not even occur to him to doubt the impression of having become suddenly deaf. When, next moment, he became sure that she was sitting up, and really very quiet, it was as though everything—men, things, sensations, had come to a rest. He was prepared to be grateful. He could not take his eyes off her, fearing, yet unwilling to admit, the possibility of her beginning again; for, the experience, however contemptuously he tried to think of it, had left the bewilderment of a mysterious terror. Her face was streaming with water and tears; there was a wisp of hair on her forehead, another stuck to her cheek; her hat was on one side, undecorously tilted; her soaked veil resembled a sordid rag festooning her forehead. There was an utter unreserve in her aspect, an abandonment of safeguards, that ugliness of truth which can only be kept out of daily life by unremitting care for appearances. He did not know why, looking at her, he thought suddenly of to-morrow, and why the thought called out a deep feeling of unutterable, discouraged weariness—a fear of facing the succession of days. To-morrow! It was as far as yesterday. Ages elapsed between sunrises—sometimes. He scanned her features like one looks at a forgotten country. They were not distorted—he recognized landmarks, so to speak; but it was only a resemblance that he could see, not the woman of yesterday—or was it, perhaps, more than the woman of yesterday? Who could tell? Was it something new? A new expression—or a new shade of expression? or something deep—an old truth unveiled, a fundamental and hidden truth—some unnecessary, accursed certitude? He became aware that he was trembling very much, that he had an empty tumbler in his hand—that time was passing. Still looking at her with lingering mistrust he reached towards the table to put the glass down and was startled to feel it apparently go through the wood. He had missed the edge. The surprise, the slight jingling noise of the accident annoyed him beyond expression. He turned to her irritated.

"What's the meaning of this?" he asked, grimly.

She passed her hand over her face and made an attempt to get up.

"You're not going to be absurd again," he said. "'Pon my soul, I did not know you could forget yourself to that extent." He didn't try to conceal his physical disgust, because he believed it to be a purely moral reprobation of every unreserve, of anything in the nature of a scene. "I assure you—it was revolting," he went on. He stared for a moment at her. "Positively degrading," he added with insistence.

She stood up quickly as if moved by a spring and tottered. He started forward instinctively. She caught hold of the back of the chair and steadied herself. This arrested him, and they faced each other wide-eyed, uncertain, and yet coming back slowly to the reality of things with relief and wonder, as though just awakened after tossing through a long night of fevered dreams.

"Pray, don't begin again," he said, hurriedly, seeing her open her lips. "I deserve some little consideration —and such unaccountable behaviour is painful to me. I expect better things. . . . I have the right. . . ."

She pressed both her hands to her temples.

"Oh, nonsense!" he said, sharply. "You are perfectly capable of coming down to dinner. No one should even suspect; not even the servants. No one! No one! . . . I am sure you can."

She dropped her arms; her face twitched. She looked straight into his eyes and seemed incapable of pronouncing a word. He frowned at her.

"I—wish—it," he said, tyrannically. "For your own sake also. . . ." He meant to carry that point without any pity. Why didn't she speak? He feared passive resistance. She must. . . . Make her come. His frown deepened, and he began to think of some effectual violence, when most unexpectedly she said in a firm voice, "Yes, I can," and clutched the chair-back again. He was relieved, and all at once her attitude ceased to interest him. The important thing was that their life would begin again with an every-day act—with something that could not be misunderstood, that, thank God, had no moral meaning, no perplexity— and yet was symbolic of their uninterrupted communion in the past—in all the future. That morning, at that table, they had breakfast together; and now they would dine. It was all over! What had happened between could be forgotten—must be forgotten, like things that can only happen once—death for instance.

"I will wait for you," he said, going to the door.   He
had some difficulty with it, for he did not remember he
had turned the key.   He hated that delay, and his
checked impatience to be gone out of the room made
him feel quite ill as, with the consciousness of her
presence behind his back, he fumbled at the lock.   He
managed it at last; then in the doorway he glanced over
his shoulder to say, "It's rather late—you know—"
and saw her standing where he had left her, with a face
white as alabaster and perfectly still, like a woman in a
trance.

He was afraid she would keep him waiting, but without any breathing time, he hardly knew how, he found
himself sitting at table with her.   He had made up his
mind to eat, to talk, to be natural.   It seemed to him
necessary that deception should begin at home.   The
servants must not know—must not suspect.   This
intense desire of secrecy; of secrecy dark, destroying,
profound, discreet like a grave, possessed him with the
strength of a hallucination—seemed to spread itself to
inanimate objects that had been the daily companions
of his life, affected with a taint of enmity every single
thing within the faithful walls that would stand forever
between the shamelessness of facts and the indignation
of mankind.   Even when—as it happened once or
twice—both the servants left the room together he
remained carefully natural, industriously hungry,
laboriously at his ease, as though he had wanted to
cheat the black oak sideboard, the heavy curtains, the
stiff-backed chairs. into the belief of an unstained
happiness.   He was mistrustful of his wife's self-control,
unwilling to look at her and reluctant to speak, for it
seemed to him inconceivable that she should not betray
herself by the slightest movement, by the very first

word spoken. Then he thought the silence in the room was becoming dangerous, and so excessive as to produce the effect of an intolerable uproar. He wanted to end it, as one is anxious to interrupt an indiscreet confession; but with the memory of that laugh upstairs he dared not give her an occasion to open her lips. Presently he heard her voice pronouncing in a calm tone some unimportant remark. He detached his eyes from the centre of his plate and felt excited as if on the point of looking at a wonder. And nothing could be more wonderful than her composure. He was looking at the candid eyes, at the pure brow, at what he had seen every evening for years in that place; he listened to the voice that for five years he had heard every day. Perhaps she was a little pale—but a healthy pallor had always been for him one of her chief attractions. Perhaps her face was rigidly set—but that marmoreal impassiveness, that magnificent stolidity, as of a wonderful statue by some great sculptor working under the curse of the gods; that imposing, unthinking stillness of her features, had till then mirrored for him the tranquil dignity of a soul of which he had thought himself—as a matter of course—the inexpugnable possessor. Those were the outward signs of her difference from the ignoble herd that feels, suffers, fails, errs—but has no distinct value in the world except as a moral contrast to the prosperity of the elect. He had been proud of her appearance. It had the perfectly proper frankness of perfection—and now he was shocked to see it unchanged. She looked like this, spoke like this, exactly like this, a year ago, a month ago —only yesterday when she. . . . What went on within made no difference. What did she think? What meant the pallor, the placid face, the candid brow, the pure eyes? What did she think during all

these years? What did she think yesterday—to-day;
what would she think to-morrow? He must find out.
. . . And yet how could he get to know? She had
been false to him, to that man, to herself; she was
ready to be false—for him. Always false. She looked
lies, breathed lies, lived lies—would tell lies—always—
to the end of life! And he would never know what she
meant. Never! Never! No one could. Impossible
to know.

He dropped his knife and fork, brusquely, as though
by the virtue of a sudden illumination he had been
made aware of poison in his plate, and became positive
in his mind that he could never swallow another morsel
of food as long as he lived. The dinner went on in a
room that had been steadily growing, from some cause,
hotter than a furnace. He had to drink. He drank
time after time, and, at last, recollecting himself, was
frightened at the quantity, till he perceived that what
he had been drinking was water—out of two different
wine glasses; and the discovered unconsciousness of his
actions affected him painfully. He was disturbed to
find himself in such an unhealthy state of mind. Excess of feeling—excess of feeling; and it was part of his
creed that any excess of feeling was unhealthy—morally
unprofitable; a taint on practical manhood. Her fault.
Entirely her fault. Her sinful self-forgetfulness was
contagious. It made him think thoughts he had never
had before; thoughts disintegrating, tormenting,
sapping to the very core of life—like mortal disease;
thoughts that bred the fear of air, of sunshine, of men—
like the whispered news of a pestilence.

The maids served without noise; and to avoid looking
at his wife and looking within himself, he followed with
his eyes first one and then the other without being able
to distinguish between them. They moved silently

about, without one being able to see by what means, for their skirts touched the carpet all round; they glided here and there, receded, approached, rigid in black and white, with precise gestures, and no life in their faces, like a pair of marionettes in mourning; and their air of wooden unconcern struck him as unnatural, suspicious, irremediably hostile. That such people's feelings or judgment could affect one in any way, had never occurred to him before. He understood they had no prospects, no principles—no refinement and no power. But now he had become so debased that he could not even attempt to disguise from himself his yearning to know the secret thoughts of his servants. Several times he looked up covertly at the faces of those girls. Impossible to know. They changed his plates and utterly ignored his existence. What impenetrable duplicity. Women—nothing but women round him. Impossible to know. He experienced that heart-probing, fiery sense of dangerous loneliness, which sometimes assails the courage of a solitary adventurer in an unexplored country. The sight of a man's face—he felt—of any man's face, would have been a profound relief. One would know then—something—could understand. . . . He decided he must have men servants. He would engage a butler as soon as possible. And then the end of that dinner—which had seemed to have been going on for hours—the end came, taking him violently by surprise, as though he had expected in the natural course of events to sit at that table for ever and ever.

But upstairs in the drawing-room he became the victim of a restless fate, that would, on no account, permit him to sit down. She had sunk on a low easy-chair, and taking up from a small table at her elbow a fan with ivory leaves, shaded her face from the fire.

The coals glowed without a flame; and upon the red glow
the vertical bars of the grate stood out at her feet,
black and curved, like the charred ribs of a consumed
sacrifice.   Far off, a lamp perched on a slim brass rod,
burned under a wide shade of crimson silk: the centre,
within the shadows of the large room, of a fiery twilight
that had in the warm quality of its tint something
delicate, refined and infernal.   His soft footfalls and the
subdued beat of the clock on the high mantel-piece
answered each other regularly—as if time and himself,
engaged in a measured contest, had been pacing together through the infernal delicacy of twilight towards
a mysterious goal.

He walked from one end of the room to the other
without a pause, like a traveller who, at night, hastens
doggedly upon an interminable journey.   Now and
then he glanced at her.   Impossible to know.   The
gross precision of that thought expressed to his practical
mind something illimitable and infinitely profound, the
all-embracing subtlety of a feeling, the eternal origin of
his pain.   This woman had accepted him, had abandoned him—had returned to him.   And of all this he
would never know the truth.   Never.   Not till death—
not after—not on judgment day when all shall be
disclosed, thoughts and deeds, rewards and punish-
ments, but the secret of hearts alone shall return, forever unknown, to the Inscrutable Creator of good and
evil, to the Master of doubts and impulses.

He stood still to look at her.   Thrown back and with
her face turned away from him, she did not stir—as if
asleep.   What did she think?   What did she feel?   And
in the presence of her perfect stillness, in the breathless
silence, he felt himself insignificant and powerless before her, like a prisoner in chains.   The fury of his
impotence called out sinister images, that faculty of

tormenting vision, which in a moment of anguishing
sense of wrong induces a man to mutter threats or make
a menacing gesture in the solitude of an empty room.
But the gust of passion passed at once, left him trembling a little, with the wondering, reflective fear of a man
who has paused on the very verge of suicide. The
serenity of truth and the peace of death can be only
secured through a largeness of contempt embracing all
the profitable servitudes of life. He found he did not
want to know. Better not. It was all over. It was as
if it hadn't been. And it was very necessary for both
of them, it was morally right, that nobody should
know.

He spoke suddenly, as if concluding a discussion.

"The best thing for us is to forget all this."

She started a little and shut the fan with a click.

"Yes, forgive—and forget," he repeated, as if to
himself.

"I'll never forget," she said in a vibrating voice.
"And I'll never forgive myself. . . ."

"But I, who have nothing to reproach myself . . ."
he began, making a step towards her. She jumped
up.

"I did not come back for your forgiveness," she exclaimed, passionately, as if clamouring against an unjust aspersion.

He only said "oh!" and became silent. He could not
understand this unprovoked aggressiveness of her attitude, and certainly was very far from thinking that
an unpremeditated hint of something resembling emotion in the tone of his last words had caused that uncontrollable burst of sincerity. It completed his bewilderment, but he was not at all angry now. He was
as if benumbed by the fascination of the incomprehensible. She stood before him, tall and indistinct,

like a black phantom in the red twilight. At last poignantly uncertain as to what would happen if he opened his lips, he muttered:

"But if my love is strong enough . . ." and hesitated.

He heard something snap loudly in the fiery stillness. She had broken her fan. Two thin pieces of ivory fell, one after another, without a sound, on the thick carpet, and instinctively he stooped to pick them up. While he groped at her feet it occurred to him that the woman there had in her hands an indispensable gift which nothing else on earth could give; and when he stood up he was penetrated by an irresistible belief in an enigma, by the conviction that within his reach and passing away from him was the very secret of existence—its certitude, immaterial and precious! She moved to the door, and he followed at her elbow, casting about for a magic word that would make the enigma clear, that would compel the surrender of the gift. And there is no such word! The enigma is only made clear by sacrifice, and the gift of heaven is in the hands of every man. But they had lived in a world that abhors enigmas, and cares for no gifts but such as can be obtained in the street. She was nearing the door. He said hurriedly:

"'Pon my word, I loved you—I love you now."

She stopped for an almost imperceptible moment to give him an indignant glance, and then moved on. That feminine penetration—so clever and so tainted by the eternal instinct of self-defence, so ready to see an obvious evil in everything it cannot understand—filled her with bitter resentment against both the men who could offer to the spiritual and tragic strife of her feelings nothing but the coarseness of their abominable materialism. In her anger against her own ineffectual self-deception she found hate enough for them both

What did they want? What more did this one want?
And as her husband faced her again, with his hand on
the door-handle, she asked herself whether he was un-
pardonably stupid, or simply ignoble.

She said nervously, and very fast:

"You are deceiving yourself. You never loved me.
You wanted a wife—some woman—any woman that
would think, speak, and behave in a certain way—in a
way you approved. You loved yourself."

"You won't believe me?" he asked, slowly.

"If I had believed you loved me," she began, passionately, then drew in a long breath; and during that
pause he heard the steady beat of blood in his ears.
'If I had believed it . . . I would never have
come back," she finished, recklessly.

He stood looking down as though he had not heard.
She waited. After a moment he opened the door, and,
on the landing, the sightless woman of marble appeared,
draped to the chin, thrusting blindly at them a cluster
of lights.

He seemed to have forgotten himself in a meditation
so deep that on the point of going out she stopped to
look at him in surprise. While she had been speaking
he had wandered on the track of the enigma, out of the
world of senses into the region of feeling. What did it
matter what she had done, what she had said, if through
the pain of her acts and words he had obtained the
word of the enigma! There can be no life without faith
and love—faith in a human heart, love of a human
being! That touch of grace, whose help once in life
is the privilege of the most undeserving, flung open for
him the portals of beyond, and in contemplating there
the certitude immaterial and precious he forgot all the
meaningless accidents of existence: the bliss of getting,
the delight of enjoying; all the protean and enticing

forms of the cupidity that rules a material world of foolish joys, of contemptible sorrows. Faith!—Love!— the undoubting, clear faith in the truth of a soul—the great tenderness, deep as the ocean, serene and eternal, like the infinite peace of space above the short tempests of the earth. It was what he had wanted all his life— but he understood it only then for the first time. It was through the pain of losing her that the knowledge had come. She had the gift! She had the gift! And in all the world she was the only human being that could surrender it to his immense desire. He made a step forward, putting his arms out, as if to take her to his breast, and, lifting his head, was met by such a look of blank consternation that his arms fell as though they had been struck down by a blow. She started away from him, stumbled over the threshold, and once on the landing turned, swift and crouching. The train of her gown swished as it flew round her feet. It was an undisguised panic. She panted, showing her teeth, and the hate of strength, the disdain of weakness, the eternal preoccupation of sex came out like a toy demon out of a box.

"This is odious," she screamed.

He did not stir; but her look, her agitated movements, the sound of her voice were like a mist of facts thickening between him and the vision of love and faith. It vanished; and looking at that face triumphant and scornful, at that white face, stealthy and unexpected, as if discovered staring from an ambush, he was coming back slowly to the world of senses. His first clear thought was: I am married to that woman; and the next: she will give nothing but what I see. He felt the need not to see. But the memory of the vision, the memory that abides forever within the seer made him say to her with the naïve austerity of a convert awed by the touch of a new creed, "You haven't the gift." He turned his back on her, leaving her completely mystified. And she went upstairs slowly, struggling with a distasteful suspicion of having been confronted by something more subtle than herself— more profound than the misunderstood and tragic contest of her feelings.

He shut the door of the drawing-room and moved at hazard, alone amongst the heavy shadows and in the fiery twilight as of an elegant place of perdition. She hadn't the gift—no one had. . . . He stepped on a book that had fallen off one of the crowded little tables. He picked up the slender volume, and holding it, approached the crimson-shaded lamp. The fiery tint deepened on the cover, and contorted gold letters sprawling all over it in an intricate maze, came out, gleaming redly. "Thorns and Arabesques." He read it twice, "Thorns and Ar . . . ." The other's book of verses. He dropped it at his feet, but did not feel the slightest pang of jealousy or indignation. What did he know? . . . What? . . . The mass of hot coals tumbled down in the grate, and he turned to look at them . . . Ah! That one was ready to give up everything he had for that woman —who did not come—who had not the faith, the love, the courage to come. What did that man expect, what did he hope, what did he want? The woman—or the certitude immaterial and precious! The first unselfish thought he had ever given to any human being was for that man who had tried to do him a terrible wrong. He was not angry. He was saddened by an impersonal sorrow, by a vast melancholy as of all mankind longing for what cannot be attained. He felt his fellowship with every man—even with that man—especially with that man. What did he think now? Had he ceased to wait—and hope? Would he ever cease to wait and hope? Would he understand that the woman, who had no courage, had not the gift—had not the gift!

The clock began to strike, and the deep-toned vibration filled the room as though with the sound of an enormous bell tolling far away. He counted the strokes. Twelve. Another day had begun. To-morrow had come; the mysterious and lying to-morrow that lures men, disdainful of love and faith, on and on through the poignant futilities of life to the fitting reward of a grave. He counted the strokes, and gazing at the grate seemed to wait for more. Then, as if called out, left the room, walking firmly.

When outside he heard footsteps in the hall and stood still. A bolt was shot—then another. They were locking up—shutting out his desire and his deception from the indignant criticism of a world full of noble gifts for those who proclaim themselves without stain and without reproach. He was safe; and on all sides of his dwelling servile fears and servile hopes slept, dreaming of success, behind the severe discretion of doors as impenetrable to the truth within as the granite of tombstones. A lock snapped—a short chain rattled. Nobody shall know!

Why was this assurance of safety heavier than a burden of fear, and why the day that began presented itself obstinately like the last day of all—like a to-day without a to-morrow? Yet nothing was changed, for nobody would know; and all would go on as before— the getting, the enjoying, the blessing of hunger that is appeased every day; the noble incentives of unappeasable ambitions. All—all the blessings of life. All—but the certitude immaterial and precious—the certitude of love and faith. He believed the shadow of it had been with him as long as he could remember; that invisible presence had ruled his life. And now the shadow had appeared and faded he could not extinguish his longing for the truth of its substance. His desire of it was naïve; it was masterful like the material aspirations that are the groundwork of existence, but, unlike these, it was unconquerable. It was the subtle despotism of an idea that suffers no rivals, that is lonely, inconsolable, and dangerous. He went slowly up the stairs. Nobody shall know. The days would go on and he would go far—very far. If the idea could not be mastered, fortune could be, man could be—the whole world. He was dazzled by the greatness of the prospect; the brutality of a practical instinct shouted to him that only that which could be had was worth having. He lingered on the steps. The lights were out in the hall, and a small yellow flame flitted about down there. He felt a sudden contempt for himself which braced him up. He went on, but at the door of their room and with his arm advanced to open it, he faltered. On the flight of stairs below the head of the girl who had been locking up appeared. His arm fell. He thought, "I'll wait till she is gone"—and stepped back within the perpendicular folds of a *portière*.

He saw her come up gradually, as if ascending from a well. At every step the feeble flame of the candle swayed before her tired, young face, and the darkness of the hall seemed to cling to her black skirt, followed her, rising like a silent flood, as though the great night of the world had broken through the discreet reserve of walls, of closed doors, of curtained windows. It rose over the steps, it leaped up the walls like an angry wave, it flowed over the blue skies, over the yellow sands, over the sunshine of landscapes, and over the pretty pathos of ragged innocence and of meek starvation. It swallowed up the delicious idyll in a boat and the mutilated immortality of famous bas-reliefs. It flowed from outside—it rose higher, in a destructive silence. And, above it, the woman of marble, composed and blind on the high pedestal, seemed to ward off the devouring night with a cluster of lights.

He watched the rising tide of impenetrable gloom with impatience, as if anxious for the coming of a darkness black enough to conceal a shameful surrender. It came nearer. The cluster of lights went out. The girl ascended facing him. Behind her the shadow of a colossal woman danced lightly on the wall. He held his breath while she passed by, noiseless and with heavy eyelids. And on her track the flowing tide of a tenebrous sea filled the house, seemed to swirl about his feet, and rising unchecked, closed silently above his head.

The time had come but he did not open the door. All was still; and instead of surrendering to the reasonable exigencies of life he stepped out, with a rebelling heart, into the darkness of the house. It was the abode of an impenetrable night; as though indeed the last day had come and gone, leaving him alone in a darkness that has no to-morrow. And looming vaguely below the woman of marble, livid and still like a patient phantom, held out in the night a cluster of extinguished lights.

His obedient thought traced for him the image of an uninterrupted life, the dignity and the advantages of an uninterrupted success; while his rebellious heart beat violently within his breast, as if maddened by the desire of a certitude immaterial and precious—the certitude of love and faith. What of the night within his dwelling if outside he could find the sunshine in which men sow, in which men reap! Nobody would know. The days, the years would pass, and . . .,

He remembered that he had loved her. The years would pass . . . And then he thought of her as we think of the dead—in a tender immensity of regret, in a passionate longing for the return of idealized perfections. He had loved her—he had loved her—and he never knew the truth . . . The years would pass in the anguish of doubt . . . He remembered her smile, her eyes, her voice, her silence, as though he had lost her forever. The years would pass and he would always mistrust her smile, suspect her eyes; he would always misbelieve her voice, he would never have faith in her silence. She had no gift—she had no gift! What was she? Who was she? . . . The years would pass; the memory of this hour would grow faint—and she would share the material serenity of an unblemished life. She had no love and no faith for any one. To give her your thought, your belief, was like whispering your confession over the edge of the world. Nothing came back—not even an echo.

In the pain of that thought was born his conscience; not that fear of remorse which grows slowly, and slowly decays amongst the complicated facts of life, but a Divine wisdom springing full-grown, armed and severe out of a tried heart, to combat the secret baseness of motives. It came to him in a flash that morality is not a method of happiness. The revelation was terrible. He saw at once that nothing of what he knew mattered in the least. The acts of men and women, success, humiliation, dignity, failure—nothing mattered. It was not a question of more or less pain, of this joy, of that sorrow. It was a question of truth or falsehood—it was a question of life or death.

He stood in the revealing night—in the darkness that tries the hearts, in the night useless for the work of men, but in which their gaze, undazzled by the sunshine of covetous days, wanders sometimes as far as the stars. The perfect stillness around him had something solemn in it, but he felt it was the lying solemnity of a temple devoted to the rites of a debasing persuasion. The silence within the discreet walls was eloquent of safety but it appeared to him exciting and sinister, like the discretion of a profitable infamy; it was the prudent peace of a den of coiners—of a house of ill-fame! The years would pass—and nobody would know. Never! Not till death—not after . . .

"Never!" he said aloud to the revealing night.

And he hesitated. The secret of hearts, too terrible for the timid eyes of men, shall return, veiled forever, to the Inscrutable Creator of good and evil, to the Master of doubts and impulses. His conscience was born—he heard its voice, and he hesitated, ignoring the strength within, the fateful power, the secret of his heart! It was an awful sacrifice to cast all one's life into the flame of a new belief. He wanted help against himself, against the cruel decree of salvation. The need of tacit complicity, where it had never failed him, the habit of years affirmed itself. Perhaps she would help . . . He flung the door open and rushed in like a fugitive.

He was in the middle of the room before he could see anything but the dazzling brilliance of the light; and then, as if detached and floating in it on the level of his eyes, appeared the head of a woman. She had jumped up when he burst into the room.

For a moment they contemplated each other as if struck dumb with amazement. Her hair streaming on her shoulders glinted like burnished gold. He looked into the unfathomable candour of her eyes. Nothing within—nothing—nothing.

He stammered distractedly.

"I want . . . I want . . . to . . . to
. . . know . . ."

On the candid light of the eyes flitted shadows;
shadows of doubt, of suspicion, the ready suspicion of
an unquenchable antagonism, the pitiless mistrust of
an eternal instinct of defence; the hate, the profound,
frightened hate of an incomprehensible—of an abominable emotion intruding its coarse materialism upon
the spiritual and tragic contest of her feelings.

"Alvan . . . I won't bear this . . ." She
began to pant suddenly, "I've a right—a right to—to—
myself . . ."

He lifted one arm, and appeared so menacing that
she stopped in a fright and shrank back a little.

He stood with uplifted hand . . . The years would
pass—and he would have to live with that unfathomable candour where flit shadows of suspicions and hate
. . . The years would pass—and he would never
know—never trust . . . The years would pass without faith and love. . . .

"Can you stand it?" he shouted, as though she could
have heard all his thoughts.

He looked menacing. She thought of violence, of
danger—and, just for an instant, she doubted whether
there were splendours enough on earth to pay the price
of such a brutal experience. He cried again:

"Can you stand it?" and glared as if insane. Her
eyes blazed, too. She could not hear the appalling
clamour of his thoughts. She suspected in him a
sudden regret, a fresh fit of jealousy, a dishonest desire
of evasion. She shouted back angrily—

"Yes!"

He was shaken where he stood as if by a struggle to
break out of invisible bonds. She trembled from head
to foot.

"Well, I can't!" He flung both his arms out, as if to push her away, and strode from the room. The door swung to with a click. She made three quick steps towards it and stood still, looking at the white and gold panels. No sound came from beyond, not a whisper, not a sigh; not even a footstep was heard outside on the thick carpet. It was as though no sooner gone he had suddenly expired—as though he had died there and his body had vanished on the instant together with his soul. She listened, with parted lips and irresolute eyes. Then below, far below her, as if in the entrails of the earth, a door slammed heavily; and the quiet house vibrated to it from roof to foundations, more than to a clap of thunder.

He never returned.

THE LAGOON

THE white man, leaning with both arms over the roof of the little house in the stern of the boat, said to the steersman—

"We will pass the night in Arsat's clearing. It is late."

The Malay only grunted, and went on looking fixedly at the river. The white man rested his chin on his crossed arms and gazed at the wake of the boat. At the end of the straight avenue of forests cut by the intense glitter of the river, the sun appeared unclouded and dazzling, poised low over the water that shone smoothly like a band of metal. The forests, sombre and dull, stood motionless and silent on each side of the broad stream. At the foot of big, towering trees, trunkless nipa palms rose from the mud of the bank, in bunches of leaves enormous and heavy, that hung unstirring over the brown swirl of eddies. In the stillness of the air every tree, every leaf, every bough, every tendril of creeper and every petal of minute blossoms seemed to have been bewitched into an immobility perfect and final. Nothing moved on the river but the eight paddles that rose flashing regularly, dipped together with a single splash; while the steersman swept right and left with a periodic and sudden flourish of his blade describing a glinting semicircle above his head. The churned-up water frothed alongside with a confused murmur. And the white man's canoe, advancing upstream in the short-lived disturbance of its own making, seemed to enter the portals of a land from which the very memory of motion had forever departed.

The white man, turning his back upon the setting sun, looked along the empty and broad expanse of the sea-reach. For the last three miles of its course the wandering, hesitating river, as if enticed irresistibly by the freedom of an open horizon, flows straight into the sea, flows straight to the east—to the east that harbours both light and darkness. Astern of the boat the repeated call of some bird, a cry discordant and feeble, skipped along over the smooth water and lost itself, before it could reach the other shore, in the breathless silence of the world.

The steersman dug his paddle into the stream, and held hard with stiffened arms, his body thrown forward. The water gurgled aloud; and suddenly the long straight reach seemed to pivot on its centre, the forests swung in a semicircle, and the slanting beams of sunset touched the broadside of the canoe with a fiery glow, throwing the slender and distorted shadows of its crew upon the streaked glitter of the river. The white man turned to look ahead. The course of the boat had been altered at right-angles to the stream, and the carved dragon-head of its prow was pointing now at a gap in the fringing bushes of the bank. It glided through, brushing the overhanging twigs, and disappeared from the river like some slim and amphibious creature leaving the water for its lair in the forests.

The narrow creek was like a ditch: tortuous, fabulously deep; filled with gloom under the thin strip of pure and shining blue of the heaven. Immense trees soared up, invisible behind the festooned draperies of creepers. Here and there, near the glistening blackness of the water, a twisted root of some tall tree showed amongst the tracery of small ferns, black and dull, writhing and motionless, like an arrested snake. The short words of the paddlers reverberated loudly between the thick and sombre walls of vegetation. Darkness oozed out from between the trees, through the tangled maze of the creepers, from behind the great fantastic and unstirring leaves; the darkness, mysterious and invincible; the darkness scented and poisonous of impenetrable forests.

The men poled in the shoaling water. The creek broadened, opening out into a wide sweep of a stagnant lagoon. The forests receded from the marshy bank, leaving a level strip of bright green, reedy grass to frame the reflected blueness of the sky. A fleecy pink cloud drifted high above, trailing the delicate colouring of its image under the floating leaves and the silvery blossoms of the lotus. A little house, perched on high piles, appeared black in the distance. Near it, two tall nibong palms, that seemed to have come out of the forests in the background, leaned slightly over the ragged roof, with a suggestion of sad tenderness and care in the droop of their leafy and soaring heads.

The steersman, pointing with his paddle, said, "Arsat is there. I see his canoe fast between the piles."

The polers ran along the sides of the boat glancing over their shoulders at the end of the day's journey. They would have preferred to spend the night somewhere else than on this lagoon of weird aspect and ghostly reputation. Moreover, they disliked Arsat, first as a stranger, and also because he who repairs a ruined house, and dwells in it, proclaims that he is not afraid to live amongst the spirits that haunt the places abandoned by mankind. Such a man can disturb the course of fate by glances or words; while his familiar ghosts are not easy to propitiate by casual wayfarers upon whom they long to wreak the malice of their human master. White men care not for such things, being unbelievers and in league with the Father of Evil, who leads them unharmed through the invisible dangers of this world. To the warnings of the righteous they oppose an offensive pretence of disbelief. What is there to be done?

So they thought, throwing their weight on the end of their long poles. The big canoe glided on swiftly, noiselessly, and smoothly, towards Arsat's clearing, till, in a great rattling of poles thrown down, and the loud murmurs of "Allah be praised!" it came with a gentle knock against the crooked piles below the house.

The boatmen with uplifted faces shouted discordantly, "Arsat! O Arsat!" Nobody came. The white man began to climb the rude ladder giving access to the bamboo platform before the house. The juragan of the boat said sulkily, "We will cook in the sampan, and sleep on the water."

"Pass my blankets and the basket," said the white man, curtly.

He knelt on the edge of the platform to receive the bundle. Then the boat shoved off, and the white man, standing up, confronted Arsat, who had come out through the low door of his hut. He was a man young, powerful, with broad chest and muscular arms. He had nothing on but his sarong. His head was bare. His big, soft eyes stared eagerly at the white man, but his voice and demeanour were composed as he asked, without any words of greeting—

"Have you medicine, Tuan?"

"No," said the visitor in a startled tone. "No. Why? Is there sickness in the house?"

"Enter and see," replied Arsat, in the same calm manner, and turning short round, passed again through

the small doorway. The white man, dropping his
bundles, followed.

In the dim light of the dwelling he made out on a
couch of bamboos a woman stretched on her back
under a broad sheet of red cotton cloth. She lay still,
as if dead; but her big eyes, wide open, glittered in the
gloom, staring upwards at the slender rafters, motionless and unseeing. She was in a high fever, and evidently unconscious. Her cheeks were sunk slightly,
her lips were partly open, and on the young face there
was the ominous and fixed expression—the absorbed,
contemplating expression of the unconscious who are
going to die. The two men stood looking down at her
in silence.

"Has she been long ill?" asked the traveller.

"I have not slept for five nights," answered the
Malay, in a deliberate tone. "At first she heard voices
calling her from the water and struggled against me
who held her. But since the sun of to-day rose she
hears nothing—she hears not me. She sees nothing.
She sees not me—me!"

He remained silent for a minute, then asked softly—
"Tuan, will she die?"

"I fear so," said the white man, sorrowfully. He had
known Arsat years ago, in a far country in times of
trouble and danger, when no friendship is to be despised. And since his Malay friend had come unexpectedly to dwell in the hut on the lagoon with a strange
woman, he had slept many times there, in his journeys
up and down the river. He liked the man who knew
how to keep faith in council and how to fight without
fear by the side of his white friend. He liked him—not
so much perhaps as a man likes his favourite dog—but
still he liked him well enough to help and ask no questions, to think sometimes vaguely and hazily in the

midst of his own pursuits, about the lonely man and the long-haired woman with audacious face and triumphant eyes, who lived together hidden by the forests—alone and feared.

The white man came out of the hut in time to see the enormous conflagration of sunset put out by the swift and stealthy shadows that, rising like a black and impalpable vapour above the tree-tops, spread over the heaven, extinguishing the crimson glow of floating clouds and the red brilliance of departing daylight. In a few moments all the stars came out above the intense blackness of the earth and the great lagoon gleaming suddenly with reflected lights resembled an oval patch of night sky flung down into the hopeless and abysmal night of the wilderness. The white man had some supper out of the basket, then collecting a few sticks that lay about the platform, made up a small fire, not for warmth, but for the sake of the smoke, which would keep off the mosquitos. He wrapped himself in the blankets and sat with his back against the reed wall of the house, smoking thoughtfully.

Arsat came through the doorway with noiseless steps and squatted down by the fire. The white man moved his outstretched legs a little.

"She breathes," said Arsat in a low voice, anticipating the expected question. "She breathes and burns as if with a great fire. She speaks not; she hears not—and burns!"

He paused for a moment, then asked in a quiet, incurious tone—

"Tuan . . . will she die?"

The white man moved his shoulders uneasily and muttered in a hesitating manner—

"If such is her fate."

"No, Tuan," said Arsat, calmly. "If such is my fate.

I hear, I see, I wait. I remember . . . Tuan, do you
remember the old days? Do you remember my brother?"

"Yes," said the white man. The Malay rose suddenly and went in. The other, sitting still outside,
could hear the voice in the hut. Arsat said: "Hear me!
Speak!" His words were succeeded by a complete
silence. "O Diamelen!" he cried, suddenly. After
that cry there was a deep sigh. Arsat came out and
sank down again in his old place.

They sat in silence before the fire. There was no
sound within the house, there was no sound near them;
but far away on the lagoon they could hear the voices
of the boatmen ringing fitful and distinct on the calm
water. The fire in the bows of the sampan shone
faintly in the distance with a hazy red glow. Then
it died out. The voices ceased. The land and the
water slept invisible, unstirring and mute. It was as
though there had been nothing left in the world but
the glitter of stars streaming, ceaseless and vain,
through the black stillness of the night.

The white man gazed straight before him into the
darkness with wide-open eyes. The fear and fascination, the inspiration and the wonder of death—of
death near, unavoidable, and unseen, soothed the unrest
of his race and stirred the most indistinct, the most
intimate of his thoughts. The ever-ready suspicion of
evil, the gnawing suspicion that lurks in our hearts,
flowed out into the stillness round him—into the
stillness profound and dumb, and made it appear un-
trustworthy and infamous, like the placid and impenetrable mask of an unjustifiable violence. In that
fleeting and powerful disturbance of his being the earth
enfolded in the starlight peace became a shadowy
country of inhuman strife, a battle-field of phantoms
terrible and charming, august or ignoble, struggling

ardently for the possession of our helpless hearts. An
unquiet and mysterious country of inextinguishable
desires and fears.

A plaintive murmur rose in the night; a murmur
saddening and startling, as if the great solitudes of
surrounding woods had tried to whisper into his ear
the wisdom of their immense and lofty indifference.
Sounds hesitating and vague floated in the air round
him, shaped themselves slowly into words; and at last
flowed on gently in a murmuring stream of soft and
monotonous sentences. He stirred like a man waking
up and changed his position slightly. Arsat, motionless and shadowy, sitting with bowed head under the
stars, was speaking in a low and dreamy tone—

". . . for where can we lay down the heaviness
of our trouble but in a friend's heart? A man must
speak of war and of love. You, Tuan, know what war
is, and you have seen me in time of danger seek death
as other men seek life! A writing may be lost; a lie
may be written; but what the eye has seen is truth and
remains in the mind!"

"I remember," said the white man, quietly. Arsat
went on with mournful composure—

"Therefore I shall speak to you of love. Speak in the
night. Speak before both night and love are gone—and
the eye of day looks upon my sorrow and my shame;
upon my blackened face; upon my burnt-up heart."

A sigh, short and faint, marked an almost imperceptible pause, and then his words flowed on, without a
stir, without a gesture.

"After the time of trouble and war was over and you
went away from my country in the pursuit of your
desires, which we, men of the islands, cannot understand, I and my brother became again, as we had been
before, the sword-bearers of the Ruler. You know we

were men of family, belonging to a ruling race, and more fit than any to carry on our right shoulder the emblem of power. And in the time of prosperity Si Dendring showed us favour, as we, in time of sorrow, had showed to him the faithfulness of our courage. It was a time of peace. A time of deer-hunts and cock-fights; of idle talks and foolish squabbles between men whose bellies are full and weapons are rusty. But the sower watched the young rice-shoots grow up without fear, and the traders came and went, departed lean and returned fat into the river of peace. They brought news, too. Brought lies and truth mixed together, so that no man knew when to rejoice and when to be sorry. We heard from them about you also. They had seen you here and had seen you there. And I was glad to hear, for I remembered the stirring times, and I always remembered you, Tuan, till the time came when my eyes could see nothing in the past, because they had looked upon the one who is dying there—in the house."

He stopped to exclaim in an intense whisper, "O Mara bahia! O Calamity!" then went on speaking a little louder:

"There's no worse enemy and no better friend than a brother, Tuan, for one brother knows another, and in perfect knowledge is strength for good or evil. I loved my brother. I went to him and told him that I could see nothing but one face, hear nothing but one voice. He told me: 'Open your heart so that she can see what is in it—and wait. Patience is wisdom. Inchi Midah may die or our Ruler may throw off his fear of a woman!' . . . I waited! . . . You remember the lady with the veiled face, Tuan, and the fear of our Ruler before her cunning and temper. And if she wanted her servant, what could I do? But I fed the hunger of my heart on short glances and stealthy words. I loitered on the path to the bath-houses in the daytime, and when the sun had fallen behind the forest I crept along the jasmine hedges of the women's court-yard. Unseeing, we spoke to one another through the scent of flowers, through the veil of leaves, through the blades of long grass that stood still before our lips; so great was our prudence, so faint was the murmur of our great longing. The time passed swiftly . . . and there were whispers amongst women—and our enemies watched—my brother was gloomy, and I began to think of killing and of a fierce death. . . . We are of a people who take what they want—like you whites. There is a time when a man should forget loyalty and respect. Might and authority are given to rulers, but to all men is given love and strength and courage. My brother said,'You shall take her from their midst. We are two who are like one.' And I answered, 'Let it be soon, for I find no warmth in sunlight that does not shine upon her.' Our time came when the Ruler and all the great people went to the mouth of the river to fish by torchlight. There were hundreds of boats, and on the white sand, between the water and the forests, dwellings of leaves were built for the households of the Rajahs. The smoke of cooking-fires was like a blue mist of the evening, and many voices rang in it joyfully. While they were making the boats ready to beat up the fish, my brother came to me and said, 'To-night!' I looked to my weapons, and when the time came our canoe took its place in the circle of boats carrying the torches. The lights blazed on the water, but behind the boats there was darkness. When the shouting began and the excitement made them like mad we dropped out. The water swallowed our fire, and we floated back to the shore that was dark with only here and there the glimmer of embers. We could hear the talk of slave-girls amongst the sheds. Then we found a place deserted and silent. We waited there. She came. She came running along the shore, rapid and leaving no trace, like a leaf driven by the wind into the sea. My brother said gloomily, 'Go and take her; carry her into our boat.' I lifted her in my arms. She panted. Her heart was beating against my breast. I said, 'I take you from those people. You came to the cry of my heart, but my arms take you into my boat against the will of the great!' 'It is right,' said my brother. 'We are men who take what we want and can hold it against many. We should have taken her in daylight.' I said, 'Let us be off'; for since she was in my boat I began to think of our Ruler's many men. 'Yes. Let us be off,' said my brother. 'We are cast out and this boat is our country now—and the sea is our refuge.' He lingered with his foot on the shore, and I entreated him to hasten, for I remembered the strokes of her heart against my breast and thought that two men cannot withstand a hundred. We left, paddling down-stream close to the bank; and as we passed by the creek where they were fishing, the great shouting had ceased, but the murmur of voices was loud like the humming of insects flying at noonday. The boats floated, clustered together, in the red light of torches, under a black roof of smoke; and men talked of their sport. Men that boasted, and praised, and jeered—men that would have been our friends in the morning, but on that night were already our enemies. We paddled swiftly past. We had no more friends in the country of our birth. She sat in the middle of the canoe with covered face; silent as she is now; unseeing as she is now—and I had no regret at what I was leaving because I could hear her breathing close to me—as I can hear her now."

He paused, listened with his ear turned to the doorway, then shook his head and went on:

"My brother wanted to shout the cry of challenge—one cry only—to let the people know we were freeborn robbers who trusted our arms and the great sea. And again I begged him in the name of our love to be silent. Could I not hear her breathing close to me? I knew the pursuit would come quick enough. My brother loved me. He dipped his paddle without a splash. He only said, 'There is half a man in you now—the other half is in that woman. I can wait. When you are a whole man again, you will come back with me here to shout defiance. We are sons of the same mother.' I made no answer. All my strength and all my spirit were in my hands that held the paddle—for I longed to be with her in a safe place beyond the reach of men's anger and of women's spite. My love was so great, that I thought it could guide me to a country where death was unknown, if I could only escape from Inchi Midah's fury and from our Ruler's sword. We paddled with haste, breathing through our teeth. The blades bit deep into the smooth water. We passed out of the river; we flew in clear channels amongst the shallows. We skirted the black coast; we skirted the sand beaches where the sea speaks in whispers to the land; and the gleam of white sand flashed back past our boat, so swiftly she ran upon the water. We spoke not. Only once I said, 'Sleep, Diamelen, for soon you may want all your strength.' I heard the sweetness of her voice, but I never turned my head. The sun rose and still we went on. Water fell from my face like rain from a cloud. We flew in the light and heat. I never looked back, but I knew that my brother's eyes, behind me, were looking steadily ahead, for the boat went as straight as a bushman's dart, when it leaves the end of the sumpitan. There was no better paddler, no better steersman than my brother. Many times, together, we had won races in that canoe. But we never had put out our strength as we did then—then, when for the last time we paddled together! There was no braver or stronger man in our country than my brother. I could not spare the strength to turn my head and look at him, but every moment I heard the hiss of his breath getting louder behind me. Still he did not speak. The sun was high. The heat clung to my back like a flame of fire. My ribs were ready to burst, but I could no longer get enough air into my chest. And then I felt I must cry out with my last breath, 'Let us rest!' . . . 'Good!' he answered; and his voice was firm. He was strong. He was brave. He knew not fear and no fatigue . . . My brother!"

A murmur powerful and gentle, a murmur vast and faint; the murmur of trembling leaves, of stirring boughs, ran through the tangled depths of the forests, ran over the starry smoothness of the lagoon, and the water between the piles lapped the slimy timber once with a sudden splash. A breath of warm air touched the two men's faces and passed on with a mournful sound—a breath loud and short like an uneasy sigh of the dreaming earth.

Arsat went on in an even, low voice.

"We ran our canoe on the white beach of a little bay close to a long tongue of land that seemed to bar our road; a long wooded cape going far into the sea. My brother knew that place. Beyond the cape a river has its entrance, and through the jungle of that land there is a narrow path. We made a fire and cooked rice. Then we lay down to sleep on the soft sand in the shade of our canoe, while she watched. No sooner had I closed my eyes than I heard her cry of alarm. We leaped up. The sun was halfway down the sky already, and coming in sight in the opening of the bay we saw a prau manned by many paddlers. We knew it at once; it was one of our Rajah's praus. They were watching the shore, and saw us. They beat the gong, and turned the head of the prau into the bay. I felt my heart become weak within my breast. Diamelen sat on the sand and covered her face. There was no escape by sea. My brother laughed. He had the gun you had given him, Tuan, before you went away, but there was only a handful of powder. He spoke to me quickly: 'Run with her along the path. I shall keep them back, for they have no firearms, and landing in the face of a man with a gun is certain death for some. Run with her. On the other side of that wood there is a fisherman's house—and a canoe. When I have fired all the shots I will follow. I am a great runner, and before they can come up we shall be gone. I will hold out as long as I can, for she is but a woman—that can neither run nor fight, but she has your heart in her weak hands.' He dropped behind the canoe. The prau was coming. She and I ran, and as we rushed along the path I heard shots. My brother fired—once —twice—and the booming of the gong ceased. There was silence behind us. That neck of land is narrow. Before I heard my brother fire the third shot I saw the shelving shore, and I saw the water again; the mouth of a broad river. We crossed a grassy glade. We ran down to the water. I saw a low hut above the black mud, and a small canoe hauled up. I heard another shot behind me. I thought, 'That is his last charge.' We rushed down to the canoe; a man came running from the hut, but I leaped on him, and we rolled together in the mud. Then I got up, and he lay still at my feet. I don't know whether I had killed him or not. I and Diamelen

pushed the canoe afloat. I heard yells behind me, and
I saw my brother run across the glade. Many men
were bounding after him, I took her in my arms and
threw her into the boat, then leaped in myself. When
I looked back I saw that my brother had fallen. He
fell and was up again, but the men were closing round
him. He shouted, 'I am coming!' The men were
close to him. I looked. Many men. Then I looked
at her. Tuan, I pushed the canoe! I pushed it into
deep water. She was kneeling forward looking at me,
and I said, 'Take your paddle,' while I struck the water
with mine. Tuan, I heard him cry. I heard him cry
my name twice; and I heard voices shouting, 'Kill!
Strike!' I never turned back. I heard him calling my
name again with a great shriek, as when life is going out
together with the voice—and I never turned my head.
My own name! . . . My brother! Three times
he called—but I was not afraid of life. Was she not
there in that canoe? And could I not with her find a
country where death is forgotten—where death is unknown!"

The white man sat up. Arsat rose and stood, an
indistinct and silent figure above the dying embers of
the fire. Over the lagoon a mist drifting and low had
crept, erasing slowly the glittering images of the stars.
And now a great expanse of white vapour covered the
land: it flowed cold and gray in the darkness, eddied in
noiseless whirls round the tree-trunks and about the
platform of the house, which seemed to float upon a
restless and impalpable illusion of a sea. Only far
away the tops of the trees stood outlined on the twinkle
of heaven, like a sombre and forbidding shore—a coast
deceptive, pitiless and black.

Arsat's voice vibrated loudly in the profound
peace.

"I had her there! I had her! To get her I would have faced all mankind. But I had her—and——"

His words went out ringing into the empty distances. He paused, and seemed to listen to them dying away very far—beyond help and beyond recall. Then he said quietly—

"Tuan, I loved my brother."

A breath of wind made him shiver. High above his head, high above the silent sea of mist the drooping leaves of the palms rattled together with a mournful and expiring sound. The white man stretched his legs. His chin rested on his chest, and he murmured sadly without lifting his head—

"We all love our brothers."

Arsat burst out with an intense whispering violence—

"What did I care who died? I wanted peace in my own heart."

He seemed to hear a stir in the house—listened—then stepped in noiselessly. The white man stood up. A breeze was coming in fitful puffs. The stars shone paler as if they had retreated into the frozen depths of immense space. After a chill gust of wind there were a few seconds of perfect calm and absolute silence. Then from behind the black and wavy line of the forests a column of golden light shot up into the heavens and spread over the semicircle of the eastern horizon. The sun had risen. The mist lifted, broke into drifting patches, vanished into thin flying wreaths; and the unveiled lagoon lay, polished and black, in the heavy shadows at the foot of the wall of trees. A white eagle rose over it with a slanting and ponderous flight, reached the clear sunshine and appeared dazzlingly brilliant for a moment, then soaring higher, became a dark and motionless speck before it vanished into the blue as if it had left the earth forever. The white man, standing gazing upwards before the doorway, heard in the hut a confused and broken murmur of distracted words ending with a loud groan. Suddenly Arsat stumbled out with outstretched hands, shivered, and stood still for some time with fixed eyes. Then he said—

"She burns no more."

Before his face the sun showed its edge above the tree-tops rising steadily. The breeze freshened; a great brilliance burst upon the lagoon, sparkled on the rippling water. The forests came out of the clear shadows of the morning, became distinct, as if they had rushed nearer—to stop short in a great stir of leaves, of nodding boughs, of swaying branches. In the merciless sunshine the whisper of unconscious life grew louder, speaking in an incomprehensible voice round the dumb darkness of that human sorrow. Arsat's eyes wandered slowly, then stared at the rising sun.

"I can see nothing," he said half aloud to himself.

"There is nothing," said the white man, moving to the edge of the platform and waving his hand to his boat. A shout came faintly over the lagoon and the sampan began to glide towards the abode of the friend of ghosts.

"If you want to come with me, I will wait all the morning," said the white man, looking away upon the water.

"No, Tuan," said Arsat, softly. "I shall not eat or sleep in this house, but I must first see my road. Now I can see nothing—see nothing! There is no light and no peace in the world; but there is death—death for many. We are sons of the same mother—and I left him in the midst of enemies; but I am going back now."

He drew a long breath and went on in a dreamy tone:

"In a little while I shall see clear enough to strike—to

strike. But she has died, and . . . now . . . darkness."

He flung his arms wide open, let them fall along his body, then stood still with unmoved face and stony eyes, staring at the sun. The white man got down into his canoe. The polers ran smartly along the sides of the boat, looking over their shoulders at the beginning of a weary journey. High in the stern, his head muffled up in white rags, the juragan sat moody, letting his paddle trail in the water. The white man, leaning with both arms over the grass roof of the little cabin, looked back at the shining ripple of the boat's wake. Before the sampan passed out of the lagoon into the creek he lifted his eyes. Arsat had not moved. He stood lonely in the searching sunshine; and he looked beyond the great light of a cloudless day into the darkness of a world of illusions.

THE END